RECORD

D0359979

MADRONA

following FLORA

NATASHA FARRANT

Dial Books for Young Readers
An imprint of Penguin Group (USA) LLC

DIAL BOOKS FOR YOUNG READERS

Published by the Penguin Group

Penguin Group (USA) LLC, 375 Hudson Street, New York, New York 10014

USA/Canada/UK/Ireland/Australia/New Zealand/India/South Africa/China

penguin.com

A Penguin Random House Company

Library of Congress Cataloging-in-Publication Data

Farrant, Natasha.

Following Flora / by Natasha Farrant.

pages cm

Sequel to: After Iris.

Summary: "Fourteen-year-old Bluebell Gadsby picks up her camera, once again, this time to document her sister Flora's budding romance with Zach, a troubled teen who happens to be Zoran's new charge"— Provided by publisher.

ISBN 978-0-8037-4128-7 (hardcover)

[1. Family life—Fiction. 2. Brothers and sisters—Fiction. 3. Dating (Social customs)—Fiction. 4. Video recordings—Production and direction—Fiction. 5. Diaries—Fiction.] I. Title.

PZ7.F2406Fo 2014

[Fic]—dc23   2013049145

Printed in the United States of America

1 3 5 7 9 10 8 6 4 2

Text set in Bembo

For Sophie, Steph, and Pierre.

Love, always.

FOLLOWING FLORA

Being a combination of conventional diary entries,
attempts at film scripts and transcripts of short films
shot by the author with the camera she was given
for her thirteenth birthday.

THE FILM DIARIES OF BLUEBELL GADSBY
SCENE ONE (TRANSCRIPT)
SUNDAY DINNNER

INTERIOR. EVENING.

The Gadsby family kitchen in the basement of the
big house in Chatsworth Square is a mess. Bubbling
pans crowd the stove. A collapsed chocolate cake
balances on top of· a fruit bowl. The sink is piled high
with dirty dishes. Water drips, steady and unnoticed,
onto the floor. FATHER sets the table, looking grumpy.
FLORA sits at one end of the sofa under the window.
She wears leopard-print leggings, an emerald-green
sweater, and the fedora she has refused to take off
since she had her hair cropped and dyed peroxide
blond last week on her seventeenth birthday. She is
reading a play. At the other end of the sofa, nine-
year-old JASMINE is her complete opposite—tiny, with
tangled black hair falling down to her waist, a long
black tunic over black jeans, and silver high-tops. She
is reading a poem called *The Raven* by Edgar Allan Poe.

MOTHER, covered in flour and melted chocolate, stands by the cooking range. She is flustered. She tastes the contents of a pan (tonight she is making goulash), burns her tongue, and throws the spoon in the sink.

NOTE 1: For the past year, Sunday night dinner has been prepared by ZORAN, the Gadsby family's au pair, who started out being able to cook nothing but sausages, but by the time he moved out a month ago he became a seriously good cook. He is coming for dinner tonight for the first time since he left to become a full-time music teacher, and Mother is determined to make an impression.

FATHER
I should be writing my book. I should not be setting tables. Remind me again why we are doing this?

FLORA
(smirks, still reading her play)
Mum wants to show us she cooks just as well as Zoran.

MOTHER

I am simply throwing together a meal for an old
friend.

FATHER

It doesn't look simple to me, it looks . . .

MOTHER

What?

FATHER

Excessive.

Mother glares at Father. For a moment, it looks like
she is going to throw the goulash at his head, but then
a football sails in through the garden door (left open
despite the cold night air because it is so hot in the
kitchen), followed by TWIG.

The football crashes into the set table and breaks several glasses.

NOTE 2: Since Twig turned eleven last summer, the family
joke is that his legs have grown so fast he doesn't know
what to do with them. And sure enough, no sooner does

Twig burst into the room after the ball than he trips over his legs, and ends up sprawled on the floor, leaving a trail of mud and wet leaves.

TWIG
(somewhat awestruck by the damage he has done)
I swear I didn't do that on purpose.

Telephone rings. Mother answers, looking increasingly dejected as she murmurs phrases like "of course I understand" and "please let us know if there is anything we can do to help."

MOTHER
(hangs up the phone, looking like she wants to cry)
That was Zoran. Someone has had a heart attack. He's not coming.

FATHER
(surveying the ruined table)
After all that?

MOTHER

David, someone has had a *heart attack.*

She notices CAMERAMAN for the first time.

MOTHER

Blue, what are you doing with that camera?

CAMERAMAN (BLUEBELL)

I'm starting up my diary again.

MOTHER

Turn it off, *now.*

SUNDAY, NOVEMBER 3

I have noticed that people only write in diaries when there's something wrong, write properly I mean. Over the past few months I've only used up about half a notebook, and most of those entries are all "I can't believe how long it's been since I last wrote" or "oh dear I feel guilty because the holidays are over and I haven't once opened this notebook," but today I have got right back into it because Mum and Dad are fighting again. Last year, when Zoran came to live with us as our au pair, we were falling apart because my twin sister, Iris, had died three years before and we still missed her so much, but things started to get better after he arrived. In fact, they improved so much that when he tried to resign last Christmas, we wouldn't let him go. Even after Mum and Dad decided to leave their old jobs so they could be at home more (Dad is a full-time writer and Mum works for a smaller makeup company that doesn't make her travel), he stayed with us right up until the summer, when he finally completed his PhD in Medieval History and told us it was time for him to move on.

"I cannot be a nanny forever," he explained when we asked him why. He has been giving music lessons all year, and now he wants to be a full-time music teacher.

At first, after Mum and Dad resigned, they made a real effort, not just with us but with each other. They stopped fighting and started to slope off for romantic weekends in the country instead. Apparently they had a lot of catching up to do, and it just wasn't possible to be romantic with four children in the house. Flora said it was a scandal. She said that at seventeen she was the one who was supposed to be skulking off to canoodle in secret, and that they were making a complete spectacle of themselves, but they were happy, so we didn't mind. And then, around about when Zoran left, Mum and Dad's canoodling stopped. This morning they had a huge fight, and they have barely spoken to each other all day. Flora says we should Resign Ourselves to the Inevitable. We were all quite ready for the parents to divorce last Christmas, and apparently the intervening months have been no more than a Temporary Reprieve.

I don't know if Zoran leaving and Mum and Dad quarreling are related. I just know that, even though he wasn't always very good at looking after us, things were better at home when he was still around.

The reason Zoran didn't come for dinner is that the grandfather of one of his students has had a stroke. The difference between a heart attack and a stroke, Dad says, is that a heart attack is what happens when blood stops flowing to the heart, and a stroke is what happens when blood stops flowing to the brain.

"So it's a brain attack," Twig said, and Dad said yes, he supposed it was.

"But why does that mean Zoran couldn't come for dinner?" Jas frowned.

"Because he was at the boy's house giving a music lesson when it happened. The boy lives with his grandfather and has no other family. Zoran offered to look after him." Mum stared at the goulash, the green beans, the potato gratin, the red cabbage with apples and raisins, the chocolate cake, and the custard and sighed.

"Those poor people," she said.

"Is the grandfather going to die?" Jas is fascinated by death. "Will the boy be an orphan?"

"I'm sure it won't come to that," Mum said. "Please stop asking questions."

"I still don't get why they couldn't come for dinner," Twig said.

Flora said, "Oh, what, Zoran should have been like, I know your only relative just nearly died but why don't you come and have dinner with a group of total strangers?"

"We're not strangers," Twig said.

"I can't imagine only having one relative," I said. "That's so sad."

As usual, nobody listened to me except for Mum, who gave me a little smile. Zoran says every family has a child who is less loud than the others, and sometimes I feel like I'm invisible. Maybe it's because unlike Flora and Jas, I don't have statement hair and clothes. My hair is brown and normal, my clothes never seem to go together, and at fourteen I'm still wearing the little round glasses I got when I was twelve, but I don't really care about any of that. I just wish once in a while someone would pay attention when I finally get a word in edgewise.

"But why is Zoran looking after him?" Jas ploughed on. "I thought he didn't want to be a nanny anymore. If he was still living with us, would that mean the boy with the grandfather would come and live here too? Couldn't they come and live here anyway?"

"STOP ASKING QUESTIONS!" said Dad.

"She's only asking because she's wants to know," said Mum.

"You just told her exactly the same thing."

"That was different."

"No it wasn't."

"Yes it was."

"Sometimes," Jas said, "I wish *I* were an orphan."

"That is a terrible thing to say," Flora scolded, but then she added that sometimes she did too, and everybody sulked for the rest of the evening.

MONDAY, NOVEMBER 4 (THE FIRST DAY OF HALF TERM)

Jake has asked me to go out with him. He left for Australia today, to go to his auntie's wedding. The holidays are only a week long, but because Australia is so far away and it is A Genuine Family Reason as well as a Highly Educational Trip, God (aka Mr. Kelly the headmaster) has given Special Dispensation for him to stay away for a month. On Friday Tom, who along with Colin is still Jake's best friend for reasons I sometimes find hard to understand, was all, "WHA-HAY, DUDE, NO SCHOOL FOR A MONTH AND THINK OF ALL THOSE HOT SURFER CHICKS," but Jake went all serious, and then this morning he said could I meet him at the Home Sweet Home café before he went to the airport, and he asked me.

Clearly, I am not invisible to Jake.

"The thought of a whole month without you," he said, "made me realize how much I like you." He asked if I would wait for him and I nearly choked over my cappuccino because, even though I've known Jake since primary school, I have never thought about him in that way, and it was the last thing I expected him to say. He taught me to skateboard last year when I was still so unhappy about Iris, and he's been one of my best friends ever since, but being best friends with someone is not the same as going out with them. I was trying to find a way of telling him that, but then he said, "Blue, are you okay?" and he looked so worried and nervous that instead I said yes, going out with him would be very nice.

As soon I got home I climbed onto the flat roof outside my bedroom window to call Dodi (it's the only place in our house where you can be really private). Dodi is about as different from me as a best friend can get. She's blond and girly, she loves fashion, and even though she's never actually had a boyfriend, she's very interested in boys.

"Tell me exactly what happened," Dodi said.

"He said, would I wait for him, and then he kissed me on the cheek and held my hand for a bit and made me promise to e-mail him every day."

Dodi sighed and said that made us practically married.

"It wasn't very passionate," I said.

Dodi says that's because we are such good friends. She says it's hard to be passionate when you know someone so well, but after a month apart, the flames of our passion will be *incandescent*.

Seriously. Incandescent. Dodi is the sort of person who has an opinion on everything. I can't imagine how it would feel to be like her, always so sure that you are right.

"So you think I should go out with him?" I asked.

"You've already said yes, haven't you?" She sounded really excited. I tried to explain about friends not being the same as boyfriends and everything, but as well as always having opinions, Dodi also often doesn't listen to me.

"You two are going to make the cutest couple," she said, but then our conversation was interrupted by my family starting to scream at each other in the garden.

"What's going on *now*?" Dodi's parents are very quiet, and she doesn't have any brothers or sisters. She is endlessly fascinated by us.

I crept to the edge of the roof. Beneath me, Dad stood by Twig and Jas's pet rats' cage, surrounded by the rest of my family, who were all yelling.

"I'll call you back," I told Dodi.

What happened was, Dad let the rats escape this morning. Normally Jas feeds them, but she was staying with her friend Lola last night, so Dad said he would do it, but then he forgot to close the cage and they ran away. Jas found the cage wide open when she came home.

Dad tried to defend himself saying the rats were probably happier living free as God intended. Jas cried, "But they are not used to the wild." Dad said Chatsworth Square was not exactly the wild, and Jas started to sob that her heart was broken forever, which is when Mum jumped in saying, "Really, David, murdering the children's pets is the last straw."

"I did not *murder* them!" cried Dad. "It was an accident! And they are rats! They can live anywhere!"

All seven of the rats have escaped. Twig, who had promised to sell Betsy's babies to his friends, informed Dad he had ruined his career. Jas cried even harder because she hadn't even realized Betsy was pregnant, but nobody was listening to her because Dad was yelling "Freedom! Freedom!" like some deranged rat revolutionary. Mum said he couldn't use political idealism as an excuse, especially applied to rats, and then he started waving his arms around crying how no one understands how difficult it is for him to be locked in his study all day trying to write a novel and knowing that the responsibility for his ENTIRE FAMILY'S WELL-BEING rested on his shoulders, and we all tiptoed away because it was clear our father had finally lost his mind.

I e-mailed Jake before writing this, to tell him all about it. Now that I have agreed to go out with him, I feel that I should tell him everything, even though it's not always easy to find the words. Nobody wants people to think their father is a lunatic. Then I called Zoran to see if he could help, but he says there is nothing he can do. Rats, once they are gone, are gone forever, in Zoran's opinion.

His student's grandfather from last night, who is called Mr. Rudowski, hasn't woken up from his stroke yet. His student, who is called Zach, is still staying with him because even though Zoran has tried to call the boy's mother, she hasn't replied.

"Zach says she lives abroad," he said.

"How come he lives with his grandfather?" I asked. Zoran said it was complicated.

"Why hasn't she replied?"

"I don't know, Blue. Believe me, I wish she would."

I wish Zoran would come home and live with us, but unlike Jas, I have no desire to be an orphan. I'd rather have two parents yelling at each other than no parents at all.

THURSDAY, NOVEMBER 7

Jas came to find me in my room this afternoon, and I knew something was up because she didn't comment on my wall, which I have spent the whole day painting from floor to ceiling with metallic silver radiator paint. This is the sort of thing you do when your grandmother, who you would normally spend half term with, decides to defy the passing of the years by going on a three-month riding holiday in Arizona. I was just working on the final coat when she slunk in (Jas, not Grandma) and said, "You have to help me."

"If I stop now," I told her, "I will forget where I got to, and the paint will be uneven. Go and ask Flora."

"Flora is at a play audition. I'm not supposed to know."

None of us are supposed to know about Flora's play auditions, because Flora is not supposed to be going to them. Flora is taking her finals in June, and all theatrical engagements are Strictly Banned.

"What about Twig?"

Jas's expression darkened.

"He's gone to have his hair cut," she sniffed.

As well as suddenly becoming tall, Twig is obsessed with how he looks. It makes Jas cross because she says he never has time to play anymore. We always used to call the two of them together the Babes, but that's all changed now, mainly because they no longer ever seem to *be* together.

"It could be worse." I tried to cheer her up. "He could be one of those boys who never wash at all."

"It's disgusting. It's all because of stupid Maisie Carter at school. He fancies her. You *have* to help me."

"I *have* to finish painting my room."

"Then I'll stay until you change your mind," she said, and she sat down on the floor.

"I'm ignoring you," I told her.

"Fine," she replied.

I stopped feeling her glare at me after a while and had almost forgotten she was there when suddenly she said, "I found two kittens in the graveyard," and I dropped my paintbrush.

There is a spray of silver paint all over my bedroom floor, but under the circumstances it hardly seems to matter. The graveyard is several streets away, and though I don't think anyone has ever told us not to go there, I'm also fairly certain it's not a place Jas should be going to on her own.

"What were you doing in the graveyard?" I asked.

"I go there quite often," she answered. "It's quiet, and there's a lovely gravestone of an old lady called Violet Buttercream where I like to sit."

"Violet Buttercream?"

Jas told me I was missing the point.

"I've hidden them in the shed," she said. "And you have to come *now.*"

So much for eternal heartbreak. I think she's already forgotten all about the rats.

SATURDAY, NOVEMBER 9

Orphaned kittens need constant attention, which is particularly difficult if you have to keep them a secret.

"Why?" I asked. "Why do they have to be secret?"

"Because they're *mine,*" she growled. "Dad would let them run away, and Twig would probably try to sell them."

"But are you quite sure they don't have a mother?"

"I've been watching them for two days. She never usually leaves them for more than a few minutes, but today she didn't come back for hours. I think something must have happened to her."

So now the kittens have a nest of their own in the shed. We plugged an electric radiator in so they wouldn't get cold, and we filled a cardboard carton with old fleeces and blankets, and then we went to the pet shop where Jas bought a litter tray, cat litter, and kitten food with money out of her savings. The kittens are the scrawniest creatures I ever saw, but they are also completely adorable. There are two of them, a boy and a girl, and they are completely black with green eyes and enormous black whiskers, which look much too big for their bodies. Jas made me take a photograph of them on my phone to show the girl in the pet shop, who says they are about twelve weeks old. She also says Jas should take them to the vet, but Jas says that's too expensive.

I don't know how long she thinks she can keep them secret. Zoran came around to see us this afternoon. He came on his new electric scooter that Flora thinks is ridiculous, but even though it normally makes him really happy, he looked so depressed when he walked in that the first thing Jas did was drag him out to the shed to show him.

"I've named the boy Ron," she said. "And the girl is called Hermione."

"They're adorable," said Zoran, but he looked really glum. We went back into the kitchen where Twig, who for reasons nobody knows is teaching himself to bake, was pulling a tray of perfect raisin and hazelnut cookies out of the oven, but even that didn't cheer Zoran up. As we ate them, Flora told us all about her audition. She is down to the last three for a small but *very important* role in a West End production, but we're still not allowed to tell the parents about it. She went through the plot, down to the minutest detail, and then she said, "All right, Zoran, what's wrong, you haven't been listening to a word I said."

"*Nobody* has listened to a word you said," Twig pointed out.

"Is that boy still staying with you?" Flora asked.

Zoran sighed and said he needed our advice. Mr. Rudowski woke up from his stroke this morning, but he can't come home yet. Instead, they are moving him out of London to a hospital in the country where they will teach him to walk and eat and sit up again, because one half of his body has forgotten how to do all these things. He has asked Zoran if Zach could carry on living with him "until other arrangements can be made."

"What other arrangements?" Flora asked.

"Until his mother gets in touch, I suppose." He explained again what he'd already told me, that he'd tried calling her but that she still hadn't replied. He also said that she and Zach had lived with her parents ever since Zach's father left them when he was little, but after Zach's grandmother died two years ago, there was a quarrel and ever since his mother and grandfather have been estranged.

"She left Zach with his grandfather and they haven't seen her since," Zoran said.

"What does estranged mean?" Jas wanted to know.

"They don't talk to each other."

"Ever?" Jas looked appalled.

"What about Zach?" Twig asked. "Does he talk to her?"

"I know they e-mail occasionally, but he hasn't heard from her either."

"What did you say to Mr. Rudowski?" Flora demanded. "Did you say you would do it?"

"Well how could I say no?" Zoran asked. "Poor kid, it's either me or a foster family he doesn't know. And I like Mr. Rudowski. He's still in mourning for his wife, and he doesn't talk much, but he's a kind old man and he's a friend of Auntie Alina's. She's the one who put us in touch."

Alina is Zoran's great-aunt, who brought him up when he came to live in England after escaping the war in Bosnia. Zoran adores her.

"So you *are* going to be his nanny." Jas's lower lip started to wobble.

"Not his nanny, exactly," Zoran said. "A seventeen-year-old boy doesn't need a nanny. More a guardian, I suppose. And just for a short time. It's not like it was with you. You do understand, don't you, Jas? He needs me."

"Like you looking after the kittens," I whispered in her ear.

Jas nodded reluctantly.

"You said you needed our advice," Flora said.

Zoran sighed, and said that he had always liked Zach, but the problem was there was a big difference between teaching a person for an hour a week and them actually living with you, and how could he get Zach to talk to him? "At the moment," Zoran said, "he barely acknowledges me at all. I understand that he's worried and angry, of course, but this morning, he wouldn't even have breakfast! He just said he wasn't hungry."

"I never have breakfast," Flora said.

"I made *pancakes*!" Zoran looked so indignant we all had to try really hard not to laugh at him. "I'm not used to not getting on with people," he said. "I thought I was good with teenagers."

"You can't lump all teenagers together, like we're all exactly the same," Flora lectured. "We're people too, you know. You can't get on with every single one of us, just because you think you're *good with us*."

"And sometimes people don't want to be helped," I added. "You can't make them talk if they don't want to."

"Is he playing in your concert?" Twig asked.

Zoran has got a load of his students working toward a sort of family concert, except us because Flora says it will be terrible, and we all secretly agree. If our own musical standard after nearly a year of lessons is anything to go by, I don't hold out much hope for his other students.

Zoran said he had asked him, but Zach had said no.

"Flatter him," Flora advised. "Boys love that. Tell him the concert will be rubbish without him."

"We'll all come to support you," I said. "We'll all cheer him like crazy and he'll feel amazing and it'll be like an unbreakable bond between you."

"Either that or everyone'll hate him, and he'll never speak to you again," Flora said.

"He's not speaking to him anyway," Twig reminded us, and Flora said that was true, so there was nothing to lose.

Zoran looked unconvinced, but said that he would give it another try.

SUNDAY, NOVEMBER 10

Today I got an e-mail from Jake in which he told me that the weather in Australia is awesome and that surfing is a bit like skateboarding but a lot more wet.

Yesterday was his aunt's wedding. They had their reception on the beach, and all the wedding guests did a giant conga in the sea, and apparently that was awesome too. He also said my e-mails are hilarious, and he reads them out loud to all his Australian relatives, who nearly died laughing over Dad releasing the rats and say my family is nuts, which I am not very happy about, because even though it's a little bit true, it's not for him to say so.

"Plus it's not very romantic," Dodi agreed when I told her. She told me I should write back straightaway and tell Jake that while I'm glad his relations find me so entertaining, our correspondence is *supposed* to be private.

"That makes it sound like I'm cross with him," I said.

"Well you *are* cross with him," Dodi replied. I said yes, but I didn't want to hurt his feelings, and Dodi said that was a little bit pathetic.

This whole boyfriend business is so complicated, and Jake isn't even in the same *country*.

TUESDAY, NOVEMBER 12

Ron and Hermione are living up to their magical names.

Today I had to go and collect Jas from Zoran's flat when I got home from school, because she ran away there after a row with Dad. Zoran called to let us know she was there.

"I don't know what is wrong with that child," Dad grumbled when I came home from school. "You all know not to interrupt me when I'm writing, but she barged in when I was right in the middle of an extremely difficult chapter, and when I asked her to leave she just stormed off. I didn't realize she'd actually left the house."

Zoran's flat is only a ten-minute walk from us, but where Chatsworth Square is all leafy and peaceful with the big communal garden in the middle, the road he lives on has shops and buses and there are always people about. He lives in a big old converted house, right on the top floor, and he has this window seat which feels like a sort of bird's nest because when you look outside you're completely surrounded by trees. I was a bit apprehensive as I walked up the stairs, thinking this would be the moment when I finally got to meet Zach, which was sort of exciting but also a bit worrying. I couldn't think what to say to him without giving away that Zoran had been talking about him behind his back. But then Zoran opened the door and I went in and the boy wasn't there and the flat looked just like it always does, with shelves crammed with books and the pictures Alina gave him when she sold her house to go into her nursing home. The radio was playing piano music, and there was the smell of Earl Grey tea and fresh paint and blue flowers in a pot, and Jas was curled up wearing one of Zoran's sweaters and wrapped in a duvet, pretending to do homework but really

23

playing with the kittens who were tumbling in and out of Zoran's guitar case next to her on the sofa.

"I don't know what you're doing here," she said. "I'm perfectly capable of walking home on my own."

"How on earth did you get the kittens here?" I asked.

"In my pockets," she said, like it was obvious.

"Your sister got caught in the rain," Zoran told me. "She was soaked to the skin when she got here."

Zoran hates it when Jas goes wandering off. He started on this whole lecture about how, in fact, Jas is still very small and has to learn to do what she is told, and how the rest of us really ought to look after her properly. He didn't even notice when Hermione rolled off the sofa, padded across the carpet, and started to climb up his trouser leg.

"It was pure luck two of my students canceled this afternoon and I happened to be in. Pure luck!" Zoran scolded.

"Where is the boy?" I asked to distract him.

"He has football practice on Tuesdays."

I curled up next to Jas and tickled Ron, who started to purr, sounding like he might just burst out of pure excitement. It's quite unbelievable that something so small can make so much noise. Then I looked round the flat again and noticed that unlike Ron, the boy Zach hadn't made his presence felt at all.

"Where are all his things?" I asked. "Can I see his room?"

"It's private," Zoran said, and then he screamed as Hermione sank her fangs into his hand and started pedaling against his wrist with her back claws.

Kitten claws are surprisingly sharp.

I know Zoran said I shouldn't, but his spare bedroom is one of my favorite rooms in the world, and I couldn't resist looking to see what it looked like with someone actually living in it. It's tiny, not much bigger than a closet. When Zoran first moved in he thought about just using it as a study or something, but then he decided that he really wanted somewhere people could come and stay, like his sister who lives in Sarajevo. So he bought a bed which fits perfectly across the width of the room under the window, and he put up hooks and shelves and even a fold-down table, painted the walls a soft pale blue like the sky, and hung those green and red glass balls you find at the seaside. It's like a ship's cabin, with a space for everything, but when I opened the door I was disappointed, because it looked exactly the same, but with clothes and schoolbooks dumped all over the floor and nothing hanging up.

"It's like he can't be bothered."

"I told you, he's not exactly overjoyed about our arrangement," Zoran said, and then he added, "I need you to take Jas and these animals home. My hand is actually bleeding."

"Is he going to play in your concert?"

"No, he is not. Apparently, he doesn't *do* concerts."

Zoran picked up Hermione so her tummy was on his hand with her little legs and her head sticking out the side so she couldn't hurt him again, and held her out to me.

"Ron just peed on your duvet," said Jas.

Zoran closed his eyes and made this little whining noise. Jas shoved Ron in one coat pocket and Hermione in the other, and we tiptoed out of the flat.

Poor Zoran. He looked so despondent when we left him, with his hands covered in scratches and his duvet covered in kitten pee, but the reason I wrote that Ron and Hermione are living up to their magical names is that when Zach got back, he found Zoran cursing and swearing as he tried to stuff his duvet into the washing machine, and he thought the whole story of the kittens so hilarious he agreed to play in Zoran's concert.

"I think he felt sorry for me," Zoran said when he called to tell us the news.

"Nobody likes cat pee," I agreed. "Did you flatter him, like Flora said?"

Zoran said that was none of my business, but I bet he did. I can just imagine them, Zach laughing his head off, Zoran choosing that exact moment to tell him how stupendously gifted he is. The thing with Zoran is he's so nice, when he wants something you never even realize what you've agreed to till it's too late.

"I suppose I should be grateful to the little beasts," Zoran said. "It's the first time I've heard Zach laugh about anything since he got here."

Jas is acting like she did the whole thing on purpose.

WEDNESDAY, NOVEMBER 13

It's weird being at school without Jake. Today in English Miss Foundry was talking about the Brontë sisters. "The Yorkshire moors!" she cried. "The tragedy of tuberculosis! The horrors of contemporary education!" except she has a lisp so it came out as *twagedy* and *houwors of contempowawy education*.

Tom asked, "Miss, how do you spell *Bwonte*?"

Miss Foundry, who is oblivious to teasing, said with two dots over the *e*.

"Exactly as I have *witten* it on the whiteboard," she said, and Tom and Colin both collapsed. I know it's mean, but it gets them every time, and there's something about the way those boys laugh. It spreads, and soon the whole class was shaking. That's when I thought of Jake. Normally there would be three of them messing about in class, but the place right in the middle of the front row where teachers always make him sit, because he is always either asleep or laughing, was empty. Suddenly I could picture exactly what would happen if he had been here, how he would have turned around and grinned at everyone behind him, like making fun of Miss Foundry's lisp was still the best joke in the world.

I do kind of miss him, in spite of his unromantic e-mails.

SATURDAY, NOVEMBER 16

Zoran came around this afternoon to ask me if I would film the concert. He said it would mean a lot to him.

"I would love to," I said, because films and their transcripts are an important part of my diaries. Ever since I got my video camera, my plan has been to record my life in words and images, but I don't often get the opportunity to film anyone other than my family.

Flora asked if he had heard from Zach's mother yet, and Zoran said that she had been in touch with her father, but there was still no news of when she was coming home.

"You should tell her about the concert," I told him. "She'd probably come for that."

Flora said, "Do you really think she'd come for Zoran's concert when she's not even been to see her father?"

"She might," I said.

Zoran said he and Zach had both written to her about the concert.

"Does *he* think she'll come?" I asked.

"That's not really for me to say," he replied.

Flora said Zach's mother sounded like a total witch.

Mum made pizza this evening for the first time in ages, which meant the kitchen was even more of a mess than usual. She was humming to herself as she cooked, with her hair full of flour. I went straight up to her when she called us down for supper and gave her the biggest hug.

"What's that for?" she asked.

"Just for being you," I said. Behind me, Twig made a puking noise, but Mum looked really happy. Then Dad came in and she went back to being cross again.

SUNDAY, NOVEMBER 17

Twig had a football match this afternoon. Mum and Dad had one of their "you go, no you go, why me, you go" arguments about it, until Flora got involved and informed them that they were *both* going, because today was his first time playing for a real team against another school.

"This is a very important day for him," she said. "So whatever is going on between the two of you, you have to get over it."

There was this moment of shocked silence, and then Mum said, "I'll get my bag," and Dad mumbled, "I'll get the car keys," and they both shuffled out behind Twig, who looked a bit startled. Twig isn't actually very good at football and I think he would have liked it better if neither of the parents had been there, but Flora says that doesn't matter.

"It's a question of principle," Flora said.

Jas, Flora, and I all went to the concert. Me to film, Flora and Jas to cheer for Zach like we had promised, and all three of us because, even though none of us will admit it, we were all dying to see what Zachary Smith looked like. The concert took place at Alina's retirement home in Richmond, where Zoran goes once a week to play the piano, and where he now also has a lot of pupils. We all piled into the drawing room, and I began to film.

THE FILM DIARIES OF BLUEBELL GADSBY
SCENE TWO (TRANSCRIPT)
THE CONCERT

INTERIOR. AFTERNOON.

The drawing room at Richmond Hill Retirement Home.
Resident students (all old) sit in armchairs arranged in
a semicircle around chairs taken from the dining room,
where nonresident students (mostly children) squirm
in the front rows with their parents behind them. JAS
and FLORA sit at the back, next to CAMERAMAN, who
is standing.

*NOTE: To keep things moving along and in order to get to
the really interesting part of the afternoon, this transcript
is skipping detailed descriptions of all the acts, which
included renditions of "Summertime," "Frère Jacques,"
Chopin's Nocturne, assorted pieces from the Music Exam-
ination Board's books for Grades One to Five, and a number of current rock songs. And then, right at the end ...*

ZORAN:

Zachary Smith on guitar, singing "Broken Birds,"
a song of his own creation.

ZACHARY SMITH stands up. Flora, Jas, and even Cameraman crane forward. He is not at all how they imag-
ined him. Medium height, slight and pale, with dark
eyes and hair falling over his face. He wears black
jeans, black high-tops, and a green-and-black checked
shirt open over an old rock band T-shirt, and his
wrists are covered in bands and bracelets. He takes his
place at the front and scans the audience, but it's clear
he doesn't find who he's looking for. His face drops
and he bends over his guitar, taking his time to tune
it. His hands are shaking. The moment seems to go on
and on. Somebody in the audience giggles. Zoran plays
a few notes on the piano and Zach rallies. He strikes a
few slow chords and begins to sing.

Broken bird in my hollowed hand
Beating heart like you want to shout
Beating hard to fight your way out
Broken bird trying to fly
Where are you going? What do you want?
Be careful the wind don't blow you about.

And the waves draw lines along the sand, the sand,

The waves draw lines along the sand,

And when they've drawn them they take them away,

I hope they take me too someday,

I hope they take me too.

Broken bird when I let you go

You mustn't look back, you mustn't, no.

Head for the sun and fly right to it,

Look for the light and go straight through it.

Don't look down or you'll fall and break,

'cause the wind ain't gonna carry you forever.

And the waves draw pictures on the sand, the

    sand, . . .

The lyrics (in Cameraman's humble opinion) are a bit sentimental, but the melody is simple and haunting and the voice—throaty, rasping but somehow also, when it hits the high notes, pure—holds the audience captive. Zachary Smith finishes. He is still for a moment, holding the silence at the end of the piece. When he looks up, it's like he's come back from a long way away and is a little bit lost.

Camera takes in Great-aunt Alina and her husband, Peter, clutching hands, rapt. Several adult members of the audience are crying. A lot of the younger kids stare with their mouths dropped open in amazement because they never thought one of their own could ever sing like that. Two older boys, whose performance of "Wonderwall" was unintentionally hilarious, look annoyed. Camera finally pans to Flora. Flora's mouth is also open, but she does not look annoyed or even amazed. Flora's eyes shine. She leans forward in her chair and she does not move, even when Zachary Smith stops singing, but keeps on looking at him like she cannot believe what she is seeing. He turns his head toward her. He catches her eye. Suddenly he doesn't look lost anymore.

He looks—amazed.

Suddenly there is nobody in the room but him and Flora.

SUNDAY, NOVEMBER 17 (CONT.)

Jas made me replay the whole concert on the train on the way home, though we skipped over most of the acts, lingering only on the kid singing "Summertime" and the old lady playing jazz tunes, until we got to Zach, and then she made me play his bit over and over again. Flora said nothing, just stared out of the train window. It was dark outside and there was nothing to see, but I don't think she'd have noticed if a herd of elephants had cantered past playing "Wonderwall" on the trumpet.

"He's not at all like I expected," Jas said. Then a little bit later she said, "I'm glad Zoran's looking after him."

Flora still said nothing.

Flora, who normally can't shut up for an *instant*. Completely silent.

It was very unnerving.

MONDAY, NOVEMBER 18

Dad found the kittens this morning or, more precisely, they found him. Somehow they got out of the shed in the night, and they were stalking up and down outside the kitchen doors when he saw them, mewing for their breakfast.

"AGGGHHHH!" Dad screamed, like they were full-grown tigers instead of thirteen-week-old kittens.

"MEEEOWWWWW!" the kittens yowled back.

"Oh my God, they're adorable!" cried Flora, clapping her hands.

"They're mine," Jas announced. "I found them starving in the graveyard, and I'm keeping them forever."

"We didn't lose the rats to make room for disease-ridden strays," Dad declared. "They will have to go."

"We didn't *lose* the rats, full stop," Flora reminded him.

"I could sell them," offered Twig.

"You could not," snarled Jas.

"This is a very bad time to have new pets," said Dad. "Your mother . . ."

"What about me?" Mum wandered down into the kitchen, and I have to say that her behavior at the moment is almost as troubling as Dad's. Normally on a Monday morning she would be tearing around in a suit, ready for work and nagging at us about being late for school, but today she was still in her robe at eight o'clock, eating peanut butter straight from the jar with her fingers.

Jas said, "It is either the kittens or me." Dad replied that there were far too many children in the house anyway. Mum walked out, slamming the door.

"That," Flora said to Dad, "is probably the nastiest thing you have ever said to any of us."

"I didn't mean it!" cried Dad. He stared from Jas to the door Mum had just stormed out of, then back at Jas again, like he couldn't decide what he should do next. Upstairs we heard another door slam. Dad yelled, "Just get rid of them!" then sprang into action and tore out after Mum.

"I did mean it!" Jas yelled after him. "I'll run away again and this time I won't come back!"

"No," Zoran said when Jas and I trudged around with the kittens this afternoon.

"Just until Daddy calms down," Jas begged.

"They peed on my duvet!" Zoran cried.

"If you don't take them," Jas said, "they will probably die."

"When are you going to e-mail me your recording?" Zoran asked. "Loads of people are asking to see it."

Jas started to scuff the carpet with her foot.

"I would love to e-mail you my recording," I said, "but the problem is I can't find my camera."

Zoran said, "What do you mean, you can't find it?" and I said, "I don't know, I've looked everywhere; it's really upsetting," and then Jas burst into tears and sobbed, "Oh, who cares about your stupid camera, what about the kittens?" Zoran hugged her but was very firm and said that he would have a word with Mum about them. He went into his bedroom to call her, but we listened at the door. It was hard to hear everything, but basically he told her how good it would be for Jas to look after two needy little animals, especially when things were a bit traumatic.

"What does traumatic mean?" Jas whispered.

"I think he means you're upset because of the rats," I whispered.

Dad is sulking but Jas is over the moon because, after talking to Zoran, Mum said of course the kittens can stay. I think possibly she only said it to annoy Dad, but this makes no difference at all to Jas.

And I've found my camera. It was under Flora's pillow.

TUESDAY, NOVEMBER 19

My sister is in love again, I wrote to Jake this evening. *She stole my camera after I filmed this boy in a concert he was in, and she ran the battery down watching my recording. I found it under her pillow. Then she went bright red at dinner when Mum asked how the concert went. I'm attaching the clip here so you can see it. Please don't show it to your family.*

I stopped to think while the clip was uploading, and then I wrote, *On second thoughts, don't take this the wrong way, but I'm not going to send this e-mail. I do hope you understand,* and then instead of pressing send I pressed delete, making today the first day since he went away that I haven't e-mailed Jake. Sometimes I have really racked my brain to think of something to write and sometimes I have written much too much, but the point is I have written every single day, just like he asked, but he hardly ever writes back and when he does it's always the same thing, about the awesome beach and how funny I am and how amazing it is that it's summer in Australia but winter over here. I told Dodi about it today during break, and she said I should write back and say it's not amazing at all, it's just that Australia is in the Southern Hemisphere and we are in the Northern Hemisphere.

It was actually Dodi who said I shouldn't write back. She says that writing back when Jake's answers are so lame makes me look like a pushover. "Like he's being rude, but you're saying it doesn't matter," were her exact words. I've never thought of it like that before, because I never expected Jake to be much good at writing, but today I did start to think that maybe she was a little bit right.

THE FILM DIARIES OF BLUEBELL GADSBY
SCENE THREE (TRANSCRIPT)
THE TROUBLE WITH CATS

EXTERIOR. MORNING.

On the lawn of the Gadsby family garden. TWIG in full
football gear, preparing to give a demonstration of his
keepy-uppy skills.

> DODI
> (in pajamas, having slept over the night before)
> Remind me again why you are doing this.

> CAMERAMAN (BLUE)
> Because I haven't done a sports video before.

> TWIG
> And to prove I can do more than Justin Murphy.

> DODI
> Who is Justin Murphy?

JAS

(also in pajamas, curled up in a deck chair draped
in kittens)

He has the highest record of keepy-uppies in
Twig's class, and he is also in love with Maisie
Carter.

DODI

Is Twig in love with Maisie Carter?

JAS

He tried baking cookies for her but apparently
she is allergic to hazelnuts.

TWIG

(glaring at Jas)

Can we just get on with it?

JAS

(smiles sweetly)

Be my guest. I'm just here to count and make
sure you don't cheat.

Twig places ball at his feet, flicks it up to his knees.
Bounces it off his right knee. Bounces it off his left

knee. He has obviously been practicing. A lot. Right, left, right, left. Right ankle. Left knee. Chest. Head. Left knee. Right knee. Jas counts each keepy-uppy. Dodi yawns loudly. Jas giggles and announces she's lost count and they have to start again. Twig tells her the whole thing is filmed anyway and they don't need her. Jas tells him one day he'll be sorry he ever said that. Twig almost drops the ball but recovers manfully with a skillful sideways flick of the left ankle. He looks triumphant but drops the ball when from the open bathroom window two stories above comes the sound of someone shouting AAAAAAAAGGGGGGGGGGGGGGG-GGHHHHHHHHHHHHHHHHHH!

> FATHER
> (his disembodied voice floating down from the window)
> Jas! JAS!! Where is that child?

Jas vaults out of her deck chair and tries to hide behind it, kittens and all.

> TWIG
> She's out here!

DODI

You're a rat, Twig Gadsby. I hope you know that.

CAMERAMAN

It's best not to mention rats in this family.

Sound of footsteps on the stairs, culminating in Father erupting into the garden, clad in nothing but a miniature towel which he holds around his waist with one hand. He marches toward Jas with his other hand extended before him, thumb and forefinger curiously pinched together, and opens them when he reaches her.

FATHER

Well?

JAS

(understandably looking like Father is deranged)
It's a black dot. Oh! It's a black dot that moves!

FATHER

It's a flea! It's a flea!! Your cats have given me fleas!!!

Dodi gasps, and almost immediately begins to scratch her head. Father yells, "You see? We've all got them!" He slaps at something on his arm, accidentally letting go of his towel. Dodi gasps again.

FATHER
TURN THAT ****** CAMERA OFF, BLUE!!

Cameraman complies, but before she does, another sound floats down from above. Picture pans up to the bathroom window, where MOTHER and FLORA stand, clutching each other, tears of laughter pouring down their faces at the sight of Father's naked bottom.

SATURDAY, NOVEMBER 23

Dad tried to order us all to clean the house after finding the fleas, but I escaped by telling him I had promised to go around to Zoran's to talk about making edits to my recording (which was true). Dodi came with me. She said she had nothing better to do, but I know that ever since she has seen him on film, she has been dying to meet Zach.

"He works on Saturday mornings," I told her. "He has a job at the old record shop on the avenue."

Dodi, who is an eternal optimist, said she was coming anyway.

Zoran said he was very pleased with my recording, and could I just cut down all the bits in between pieces, the applause, and the tuning up, and so forth, to make it a little bit shorter.

"Oh, and take out that bit with Flora and Zach," he added. "There's far too much footage of them looking at each other."

Dodi protested that was the best bit. Zoran said it was inappropriate.

"You *can't* get rid of that footage," Dodi said as we ran downstairs. "It would be criminal. It would be a waste. It would be a *criminal waste.*"

And then we both stopped talking, because *he* was coming up the stairs toward us.

Zachary Smith.

Who Flora's in love with.

He stopped in front of us. "Oh," he said. Then, "You're the one with the camera."

"She is indeed," Dodi drawled when I couldn't think of an answer.

"With the kittens," said Zach.

"They're my little sister's."

"Cool," he stammered. And then he looked embarrassed

and mumbled about having forgotten something and being late for work, and ran off up the stairs.

"Very, very odd," commented Dodi.

"Most peculiar," I agreed.

"Do you think he was trying to charm you? Like he's hoping you'll tell Flora how dreamy he is, and what witty conversational skills he has?"

We both sniggered at that. I know it's not nice.

Dodi says she's disappointed in Zach in real life. She says that when he's not singing or casting smoldering looks at Flora, he looks like a bit of a loser. I said that he reminds me of the poet Keats, who we studied in English before the Bwontës, and who died tragically young in Italy of tuberculosis. Dodi, who never lets anything she learns at school follow her into real life, said she would never have thought about that but that she supposed he did remind her of all sorts of doomed rock stars, and perhaps that is what Flora saw in him.

Dad has spent the whole day cleaning. The house is draped with drying bed linen from basement to attic, and I have never seen it sparkle so much. At dinner, he announced again that we had to get rid of the kittens, but Mum said no.

Dad said the kittens kept disturbing him when he was trying to work.

"In this family," Mum said, "we look after the weak and the vulnerable. In fact," Mum added, "we don't just look after them, we *welcome* them." She sounded really fierce, and also like she wasn't really talking about kittens at all. I think Dad realized that too, because he didn't answer but looked down when she glared at him.

The kittens have been rolled in flea powder like two little doughnuts in icing sugar, and they are not allowed out of the kitchen.

THE VERY MUCH ENHANCED FILM DIARIES OF BLUEBELL GADSBY
SCENE FOUR (TRANSCRIPT)
LOVE AT FIRST SIGHT

INTERIOR. AFTERNOON.

ZACHARY SMITH sits on a chair, playing his guitar. His
surroundings (the Richmond Hill Retirement Home)
have vanished in a misty haze. All background noise
has been edited out. The only sound is that of his
singing and strumming. Picture cuts to FLORA, gazing
at him. A ribbon of pink cartoon hearts floats from
her mouth to form a bubble above her head, inside
which, in yellow letters, is the single word SIGH. Zach,
in his misty haze, is enveloped in a cloud of baby blue
songbirds. Think Disney's Cinderella and all the little
animals. His speech bubble says, YOU'RE BEAUTIFUL.
When the song reaches the chorus—*and the waves draw
lines along the sand, the sand*—picture switches briefly
to a tropical sunset, and a couple running together in

the water, then returns to a split screen with Zach on one side, looking poetically tragic, and Flora on the other, smiling with her eyes closed in apparent ecstasy. Picture melts away as music fades and the following words take over the screen:

ZACH AND FLORA
LOVE
AT
FIRST
SIGHT

SUNDAY, NOVEMBER 24

It was all Dodi's idea. I'm not saying I didn't want to go along with it, and that I'm not glad I did. We spent the whole day turning Zach and Flora gazing at each other at the concert into a full-length music video. I learned a ton of things. The end result was fabulous.

It just wasn't my idea to put it on YouTube.

Flora has a history with YouTube. Last year, her then horrible boyfriend's even more horrible friends uploaded a film of Flora playing one of Snow White's seven dwarves in a Christmas show, when her leather shorts split as she was doing a forward bend. It was a very poor quality video, but it was unmistakably Flora, and she was unmistakably not wearing anything under the shorts.

"But this is not humiliating at all," Dodi reasoned. "This is tasteful and romantic." And then she said that our clip could be seen by millions of people, and that this could be the beginning of a whole new career for me as a director of pop videos.

"I'm not sure that I *want* a career directing pop videos," I said. "I want to do something meaningful, like make undercover documentaries exposing crime and corruption. Or award-winning nature programs. And one day, feature films. I'm not sure pop videos are really my thing. And anyway, someone sitting on a chair playing the guitar hardly counts as a pop video, even with little birds and love hearts and butterflies . . ."

"Stop being such a dork." All the time I was talking, Dodi was fiddling with the computer.

"All done," she said when I finished explaining. "At the very least it will make him and Flora realize how much they fancy each other."

"Flora will kill me," I said. "Zach will kill me. *Zoran* will kill me."

"Not when Zach sweeps her off her feet and declares his undying love, they won't. Then Flora and Zach will be eternally grateful, and Zoran will actually thank you, because Zach will stop being so tragic."

That is Dodi's point of view.

Me, I just hope Flora never, ever sees it.

TUESDAY, NOVEMBER 26

Mum and Dad left home together early this morning. I was brushing my teeth at the bathroom window and I watched as they got into the car and then just sat there, side by side in the front seats, talking for ages but not looking at each other. Even when Dad leaned over and kissed Mum on the cheek, she just carried on staring out of the window, and I'm pretty sure she was crying.

"They've gone to the doctor," said Jas on the walk to school. "I looked in her diary."

"But why has Dad gone with her?" I asked. Jas shrugged and said the diary didn't say why.

"It can't be serious," Flora said. "Dad would be nicer to her if it was."

"I saw him kiss her," I reminded her.

"Well, that makes a pleasant change." Flora never worries about *anything* unless she absolutely has to.

Film club was canceled after school today, so I came

home early. The house was dark when I got back and at first I thought that it was empty, but when I went to the kitchen to make some tea the back door was open and Mum was sitting on the veranda, wrapped in a blanket and staring at the garden. I called out to her and she jumped. When she turned around I saw that she was holding a photograph.

"What are you doing?" I asked her, and she said, "Nothing!" with that smile we all hate because it is so fake. She moved over on the bench to make room for me to sit down. The photograph fell off her lap. It was a picture of Iris.

"Oh," I said, and after that we sat very still and silent. The kettle boiled and I got up to make us both some tea. When I got back the photograph was gone, and Mum had that look people get when they were about to cry but then managed to stop themselves. She took the mug I offered her. I sat on the floor with my back to her chair, and we both watched the garden, which at this time of year is basically muddy and brown except for a few roses still clinging on like nobody's told them yet that it's nearly winter.

"Something momentous is happening," Mum said.

I thought of the photograph, and of Iris, and of this morning's secret doctor's appointment.

"Are you going to die?" I tried not to let my voice shake. Mum smiled and kissed me.

"I'm not planning on it," she said.

. . .

"She's not planning on it?" Jas cried this evening when I told her. "What does that even mean?"

I said I didn't have a clue.

"What if Flora's wrong?" Jas asked. "What if it *is* serious?"

"I'm sure it isn't," I said, but I am not like Flora, and neither is Jas. If something is wrong, we would rather know about it.

WEDNESDAY, NOVEMBER 27

My video has had thousands of hits! I can't give an exact number because people keep looking at it, but Dodi is beside herself with excitement and I would be too if so many people weren't furious with me.

What happened was this: On Monday night, a girl in Tennessee with about a million followers on Twitter tweeted about it, posting a link to the video.

A whole bunch of her followers retweeted it.

A girl Flora used to know, who goes to Zach's school, read the tweet, saw the video, and posted it to Facebook and Instagram, then retweeted it and texted and e-mailed the link to everyone in her address book, including Flora's best friend, Tamsin. By morning break, pretty much every-body in both schools had seen it.

Flora has not responded well to global celebrity.

U. Hve. Ruined. My. Life.

That was her immediate reaction on discovering she was famous. She sent it via text ten minutes into first period, just after Tamsin showed her the video on her iPhone.

I am litrly gonna mrder u. Flora is the world's fastest texter. *I will nvr forgive u.*

"Ignore her," Dodi whispered when I showed her my phone under the desk. *Every1 is laughing at me. Graham keeps singing at me. I am going 2 tear u lmb from lmb.*

"Can I come and live with you for a bit?" I whispered back to Dodi.

U r no lnger my sister! Once I hve kld u I am nvr, evr gonna spk 2 u again. Prepare for yrs of misry.

That's when Madame Gilbert confiscated my phone, which, quite frankly, was a relief.

Zach's response to his newfound fame has been to get into a fight. A load of people in his class were teasing him, and when they didn't stop he threw a punch at one of them, and then a whole bunch of boys got involved until their teacher came in. Someone in his class filmed the whole thing and posted that on Facebook as well. It got taken down later, but not before everyone was talking about it. Zach got sent home and has been suspended till the end of the week, and Zoran is even more furious with me than Flora is. In fact he came around this afternoon just to shout at me.

"I asked you to delete that scene!" he yelled. "Not post it all over the Internet like some dating agency advertisement!"

I said I was really, really sorry.

"You knew how much that concert meant to him, Blue. He poured his heart and soul into that song, and then you . . ."

"I'm *sorry*," I said again.

"And now he's in trouble at school. I had to go in this afternoon to make all sorts of excuses for him about extenuating circumstances. His *sick grandfather*. His *missing mother*. And you make fun of him!"

I started to cry. Zoran sighed, and sat down next to me on the bed.

"You have so much talent," he said quietly. "It makes me mad to see you waste it."

"It was Dodi's idea," I sniffed.

"You have your own way of looking at the world, Blue. You see things other people don't. That's why you like filming, and writing. You pick up on things. You don't need to hide behind people like Dodi."

"Dodi's fun," I said.

"And you are serious."

"I don't want to be *serious.*"

"Serious people can do great things." He nudged me with his elbow and pulled a sad, serious face. "Stop to think before you do something like this again, okay?"

I looked at my films again after he'd gone. Mum and Flora laughing together at the bathroom window, Alina and Peter holding hands at the concert, Jas in the garden draped in kittens—is this what Zoran means about picking up on things? Because if I posted those on YouTube, I bet they wouldn't get viewed by thousands. For a moment, I felt annoyed with Zoran because it feels like quite something to have so many people looking at what I've done. Then Jake sent me a message on Facebook to tell me Tom had sent him the link to my video and all his family were laughing their heads off about it in Australia, and I immediately felt bad again.

It's not funny, I wrote back.

Jake wrote, *lol.*

I wrote that I didn't think he understood the seriousness of the situation, and when was he coming home anyway?

Jake wrote, *Sunday,* and man, he didn't want to leave because Australia was so awesome.

I didn't reply.

The atmosphere at home is horrible, and this time it's all my fault.

"The most logical thing," Dodi said today, "is to get Zach and Flora together."

"In what way is that remotely logical?" I asked.

We were in our kitchen after school, eating Twig's latest batch of banana and chocolate chip cookies.

"It's what we planned to do all along," Dodi said. "It makes Zach happy; it makes Flora happy; it makes Zoran happy, plus now it lets you off the hook. It's the perfect solution."

"But how?"

"We finish what we started!" Dodi cried.

"How?" I repeated, and Dodi admitted she didn't know.

"Think!" she ordered. We sat there for ages, munching and thinking. We finished the banana and chocolate chip cookies, and moved on to jam and coconut, until we eventually came up with this:

Stalk Zach.

Establish his routine.

Take Flora to a place their paths will cross.

Run away.

Which is rubbish, I pointed out to Dodi, for loads of reasons but mainly because even if we do manage to work out where Zach is going to be, Flora is about as likely to follow us there as she is to crush a kitten with her bare hands.

"We need help," concluded Dodi. "But who?"

We stared out at the garden. Twig has finally convinced Dad to help him build a tree house in the garden, but Dad has already given up, so now Twig and Jas were out there together, trying to finish it on their own and yelling at each other.

"There's our answer," Dodi said.

"You only talk to us when you need something," Jas said when we told her what we wanted her to do. "It's rude."

"You could pay us," Twig suggested.

"You are obsessed with money," I told him. Twig shrugged and said to blame the parents and their imminent separation. He said it's a well-known fact families are poorer when they divorce.

"Don't you want Flora to be happy?" asked Dodi.

"Not particularly," said Jas, but money did it in the end.

"What if he is too embarrassed to talk to her?" Jas asked.

"I would be, after that video," Twig sniggered.

"Everything will work out just fine," I said firmly.

Twig says he has never heard of a plan with so much potential for failure, but it hasn't stopped him taking my money. Operation Flora is costing me five pounds a head for him and Jas, plus expenses, "in case we have to buy anything while we are out."

Things started to go wrong from the beginning when Flora refused to take the Babes shopping, claiming excessive fame.

"I can never show my face in public again," Flora said. "It's all Blue's fault. She can take you."

"I have homework," I said.

"Surely," Flora said, "they are old enough to go on their own."

"I am very, very young," said Jas. "And Twig is extremely irresponsible."

"I'll take you," said Mum from the sofa where she was lying, and we all jumped because we thought she was asleep.

"You mustn't!" I cried. Mum looked startled. "You're so tired," I said. "And you don't look well."

"I do feel a little sick," she admitted.

My heart dropped. Jas and I looked at each other. Mum still hasn't told us why she went to the doctor and neither of us has had the courage to ask.

"Oh for goodness' sake," sighed Flora. "Just let me find my biggest hat and sunglasses."

Dodi and I followed them at a discreet distance. We stopped just inside the park, out of sight but close enough to the shops to get there within minutes of Twig texting us.

Later, Twig told me exactly what happened. The plan

continued going wrong when instead of heading straight to the bookshop, like she was supposed to, Flora dived into a clothes shop then bumped into Tamsin, who suggested they go for coffee. Jas dragged her away but when they finally got to the record shop, Zach wasn't there.

"He left early," Twig texted.

"Well where the ★★★★★★ ★★★★ is he then?" I said to Dodi.

"Over there," she replied.

Right in front of us, across the lawn on the basketball courts. Shooting hoops and looking moody, all on his own.

After that, things moved very fast.

I texted Twig back to tell him where we were.

Jas announced that vinyl records were a waste of time, especially since we don't have a record player, and that she wanted to go to the park.

Flora, who was enjoying herself, said tough.

Jas ran away.

Flora ran after her.

Twig, after a quick text to me, followed.

"They will be here in about two minutes," I informed Dodi.

"Which will be too late!" she hissed. "He's leaving!"

It was true. Zach had tucked his basketball under his arm and was lolloping—I swear, he lollops—away from us across the court.

Dodi grabbed my hand.

"Come on!" she cried, and started running.

So there we were. Flora, Jas, and Twig running down the main street. Dodi and me tearing after Zach. Zach, unaware of any of us, lolloping.

"How are we going to stop him?" I panted.

"Leave it to me," she gasped.

We drew level with Zach. Dodi threw herself at his feet.

"I'm sorry!" she cried "We weren't laughing at you! We never thought so many people would watch the video!"

Zach just stared at her.

"Forgive us!" Dodi begged.

"Dodi." I nodded toward the park entrance. Jas and Twig were streaking across the lawn toward us, trailing.

"We have to go!" Dodi shouted. And then me and Dodi ran away, except we were laughing so much we had to run with our legs crossed so as not to pee.

Zach just carried on staring. He stared as we vanished down the path and dived into a bush, and he stared some more as Jas and Twig shot past and followed us, and then he stared and stared and stared as Flora, red and breathless and still wearing her hat and sunglasses, erupted onto the court, screeched to a halt, and stared back.

The four of us huddled together in the bushes and watched.

"This plan was catastrophic," I said.

"I did warn you," said Twig.

"They're talking!" cried Jas.

She was right. We were too far away to hear what they were saying, but they were *definitely* talking. Flora and Zach, face-to-face on the basketball court. He shuffled his feet, tossing his ball from one hand to the other. She tucked her hair behind her ear. He pointed down the path to where we were hiding. Flora turned as if to go. Zach put his hand out, like he was asking her to stay. And she did.

"Bingo," whispered Dodi.

"Time to go home," I agreed.

We crept out of the bushes and went the long way around the park so as not to disturb them.

It was almost dark by the time Flora got home. She didn't mention the fact that Twig and Jas had run away, and nobody asked her where she'd been. But tonight I heard her humming Zach's song to herself in the bathroom, and I think that tomorrow she may start talking to me again.

SUNDAY, DECEMBER 1 (VERY EARLY IN THE MORNING)

Tomorrow, or rather today, started almost before yesterday ended, and Flora is already talking to me. I was asleep about five minutes when something landed on the end of my bed, and when I opened my eyes that something was her.

"Are you awake?" she whispered.

"No," I mumbled.

"So I met Zach."

Flora giggled, and stretched out at the end of my bed with her feet dangling over one side and her head hanging down over the other.

Before today, I never really thought much about love at first sight. It's just one of those things you assume must be true because films and books are always going on about it, but Flora is my first real life experience with it, and it's extremely strange. She's had about a million crushes and boyfriends before, but this is the first time she has come into my bedroom in the middle of the night to talk about it.

"He's so gorgeous," she said. "I mean, close up. He's got these amazing brown eyes, and when he smiles his mouth goes up a little bit more on one side than the other, which is adorable, and he has a dimple in his left cheek. And he's really funny. I apologized about you and your video. I mentioned, you know, the fight thing, and he got all embarrassed and said he didn't normally go around punching people. He said that song was very personal to him, and it upset him seeing it taken apart like that. He's so sensitive and artistic. He said he had a lot on his mind, and I said

I knew a bit about it through Zoran, but discreetly, you know, like I didn't mention his witch mother not coming to the concert or anything. I just said very vaguely about his grandfather and how I was sorry, and he was all yeah, well, it was tough but he didn't want to talk about it, and then it was a tiny bit awkward but he asked if he could see me again!"

"Your face is going red," I said. "I think the blood must be going to your head."

Flora flipped back the right way up and beamed at me.

"Did I tell you he smells delicious? Like lemons. Or maybe limes."

"That's so lovely."

"I'm going back to bed now."

She glided over to the door in a sort of weird improvised ballet and drifted out.

I have been lying awake for ages. Jake comes home today. I realize that I have absolutely no idea what he smells like.

SUNDAY, DECEMBER 1 (CONT.)

If I was making a film about me and Jake, I would call it something like *The Saga of Bluebell and Jake*, and it would go like this:

64

THE SAGA OF BLUEBELL AND JAKE
THE DAY HE CAME HOME

BLUE, looking casually elegant without her glasses,
sits on a park bench gazing wistfully at the duck pond.
JAKE appears soundlessly behind her.

> JAKE
>
> You are even more beautiful than I remembered.

Blue turns toward him with a dainty sob. Jake folds
her in his manly arms.

> BLUE
>
> Jake! How delicious! You smell exactly like
> cinnamon toast!

Or this: BLUE walks down the street with a group of
friends, carefree and laughing, when they run into
JAKE, hurrying toward them, carrying a bunch of flowers and a haunted expression.

JAKE

(his voice choked with emotion)

Thank God you're alive! I've been trying to call you every day since your last witty and amusing e-mail to apologize for sharing it with my entire family!

BLUE

Madame Gilbert confiscated my phone!

JAKE

(folding her in his manly arms)

Your eyes are like the ocean on a summer's day, and your fragrance reminds me of roses.

I know both of these would be super cheesy, but I still think they would be better than what actually did happen today, which was—nothing.

I waited all day for Jake to call. I don't even know why I got so worked up about it. Maybe it was Flora last night, like all that head over heels stuff was contagious. Maybe I do like him more than I thought. Or maybe it was just Dodi, turning up at the crack of dawn with her hair curlers and a bag full of makeup, making me feel like it was all a much bigger deal than it was.

"You have to be dazzling," she scolded when I tried to resist her makeover. She made me steam and exfoliate my face, then started to turn my dead straight hair into droopy ringlets.

"They're pretty and feminine," she said.

"They're hideous," I retorted, but Dodi said I had to trust her.

"I'm going to leave you the makeup and the curlers," she said, after painting my nails pink and showing me how to make up my eyes. "Make sure you get up early tomorrow morning to use them. And if Jake comes around, put on just a tiny bit of lip gloss. You don't want him to think you're trying too hard."

"My hair is *curly*," I said, but she said that was different.

The more he didn't call, the more I wished he would. After Dodi had gone, I sat down at my desk and did my homework. I worked all afternoon and I tried not to jump every time I heard a telephone or the doorbell ring, and when Dodi called this evening for an update I pretended I didn't care, but I do. At least, I *think* I do.

If I wish Jake would call me, it means I really like him—doesn't it?

If Iris were here, she would laugh at the lot of us—Dodi

being bossy and Jake's rubbish e-mails and me being so nervous. Even though she died way before any of us were into boys, I know she would have made me feel better. It's December today. For most people that means Christmas and holidays, but for me it's the month when she died, and right now the only thing I'm absolutely certain about is how much I miss her.

MONDAY, DECEMBER 2

Dodi gave me precise instructions about what to wear today, but I overslept, and then I realized all my tights have holes in them so I couldn't wear my new puffball skirt like she said I should, and my jeans were all in the wash so all I had were some old dungarees that make me look like I'm about nine years old. Flora said I looked like an extra on a farming program but by then it was eight and I had to run to get to school on time.

Dodi looked disapproving as I slid in next to her in assembly. "You're red," she said. "You haven't done your hair and you're not wearing any makeup. Also, you're sweating."

"Is he here?" I panted.

"Two rows down, right at the end," she sighed. "And what's with the farm girl look?"

"It's only Jake," I said, but my heart was hammering. From where I was sitting, I could just see the back of his head. Tom and Colin were jostling him. Jake turned round and smiled this little smile, and I saw that he is looking very brown and fit from his holiday. I admit that is not what I was expecting. In my mind he was still what he always was before he went away, which was more pale and interesting. "Only Jake," Dodi smirked.

Dodi says that Jake has come home hot. I don't know how I feel about this. It's difficult enough coming to terms with the whole idea of having a boyfriend at all, let alone a hot one, and I think Jake is maybe a bit confused too. He bought me a bush hat with corks hanging from it and a boomerang, which are nice but hardly romantic. Then later, when we were walking home with the others, he barely said a word. I thought that maybe we would stop in the park or he would ask me over to his place, like he used to do sometimes when we were just friends, but when we reached our usual crossroads all he said was "See you tomorrow, Blue," and we went our separate ways.

I think this may all be a giant mistake.

I ran into Flora on the way home. She and Zach both had free periods this afternoon, and she was all aglow with love after meeting up with him at Home Sweet Home. Jas was sitting on her own in the kitchen when we got in, surrounded by notebooks, and I think she found Flora as irritating as I do because she took one look at her and grumbled that her whole family was obsessed with romance.

"Grumpy!" Flora caroled. "Where's Twig?"

Twig, Jas informed us, had gone straight from school to the railway bridge by the canal, to look at the trains passing underneath.

"Maisie Carter has a little brother," she spat. "Maisie's little brother likes trains. Maisie was supposed to look after him after school today, but she had better things to do, so she asked Twig to take him to look at the choo-choos."

"That's so sweet," said Flora.

Jas said she thought it was revolting.

WEDNESDAY, DECEMBER 4

Dodi says that Jake isn't behaving like a proper boyfriend should. He doesn't wait for me after lessons or talk to me on my own or behave like anything between us is at all different. She thinks he's trying to avoid me. Like today there was only him and me and Dodi at lunch, because Tom and Colin had detention, and Dodi said, trying to leave us alone, "I have to go to the library now to research population density in the Sahara," and instead of staying with me he said he had homework to do too, and we all ended up going together.

"It's not what you want in a boyfriend," Dodi said. She says she is going to talk to him and explain the basic rules of going out with people.

I told her what I thought about it all being a giant mistake.

"I think actually we may not be going out anymore and he just hasn't told me," I said.

"Holding hands," Dodi went on, not listening to me again. "Going on dates. Spending time together. *Kissing.*"

"I'm not sure I'm ready for any of those things," I said, but Dodi says of course I am.

THE SAGA OF BLUEBELL AND JAKE
THE KISS
(OR, UTTER HUMILIATION)

EXTERIOR, DAY.

JAKE and BLUE walk home along a London street in awkward silence.

> JAKE
> (staring at the pavement)
> So, d'you want to go to the cinema or something?

> BLUE
> (examining the bark of a tree)
> I, um, er, gah.

> JAKE
> (apparently not noticing that Blue is dying, strangled by her own embarrassment)
> Saturday afternoon?

BLUE

Hem, er, goo, agh.

JAKE

Right, well see you tomorrow then.

He pounces and presses his mouth against hers. She
makes a choking sound and runs away.

THURSDAY, DECEMBER 5

And that was it. My first proper kiss.

I don't know what Dodi said to Jake, but we were all
hanging around outside the sweet shop together after school
when the others just *vanished*, and the whole pounce/kiss/
running away thing happened.

The film of my life is not even a tragedy. A tragedy is
Romeo and Juliet or *Titanic*, where everybody dies. My life
is barely even a romantic-comedy. At best, it's reality TV,
except sometimes it doesn't even feel real.

"What's it like when you kiss Zach?" I asked Flora when
she breezed in this evening.

"Like it's none of your business," she replied.

"But really."

And Flora is truly in an exceptionally good mood at the moment because instead of saying what I fully expected, which was "I don't have time to instruct inferior sisters in the art of love," she went all dreamy.

"Magic," she sighed. "Like we're the only two people in the whole world, and everything is still, like time has stopped but is spinning really fast at the same time. And warm. Like coming home. Like there's nowhere else I ever want to be." She was sort of staring into space, but then she gave herself a little "ah well, back to the real world" shake and said, "Why, what's it like with Jake?"

"We're not really into that sort of thing," I said.

"What, like *kissing*?" she said, and then thank God Jas came into my room and said, "Can I ask you something?"

"You're covered in ink," Flora said as she left. "I swear I never worked that hard in primary school."

Jas ignored her. "I need you to help me," she told me. I said the last time she asked me to help her we all ended up combing our hair for fleas.

"I'm not in the mood," I told Jas. "I am thinking important thoughts, and I need to write them down."

Kissing Jake did not feel remotely like coming home.

Kissing Jake felt wet and odd and not at all how a first kiss ought to.

FRIDAY, DECEMBER 6

Today before going to work Mum put all the laundry in the bin instead of the washing machine. When she came home this afternoon, she realized what she had done, and sat down in the middle of the kitchen floor and cried. Then Dad came in to find out what all the noise was and sat right down on the floor beside her.

"I didn't like those shirts anyway," he said. Mum started to laugh and threw her arms around his neck, and then they went to bed. We haven't seen them since, except when Dad came down to make grilled cheese because Mum was hungry. He got a text while he was making it, and it was from Mum in the bedroom telling him she wanted Rice Krispies as well. I haven't seen him laugh so much *ever*. I didn't even know Mum liked Rice Krispies.

SATURDAY, DECEMBER 7

Zach was working today, so Flora couldn't go and see him, but apparently if she isn't with him she has to talk about him *all the time*. She hardly stopped all day.

"He hasn't seen his mother for *over two years*," she told us. "You know I used to think she was a witch? Well, it turns out nice Mr. Rudowski threw her out after his wife died and told her to never come back. Zach's never forgiven him for it."

"That sounds very dramatic," Mum said. She was tired again. Jas and I were sitting on her bed playing cards with her to keep her company, while Flora went on about Zach and Twig practiced hairstyles in the bathroom.

"It's true!" Flora insisted. "Zach says she was a brilliant mum. She used to do things like take him out of school to go to the seaside, or camp overnight in Richmond Park. One time she took him for tea at the Ritz and wore a long gold cocktail dress and made him pretend she was the queen of Narnia."

"She sounds funny," Jas said, shuffling cards. "Why don't you ever do anything like that, Mummy?"

"She sounds weird," I said. "And if she's so brilliant, how come she isn't here now?"

"She lives in the South of France now. Zach really, really wanted her to come to his concert, and she wrote and told him she would try, but he thinks she didn't come because she's so scared of his grandfather."

"His grandfather who's in hospital?" I said.

Flora said she didn't see what difference that made, and why was her family always so unsupportive when she tried to tell them things, and then Dad came in and said, "Personally, I'm a little worried about this young man."

"Were you *listening*?" Jas looked impressed. "Like *spying*?"

Dad said he'd seen the video of Zach fighting in his classroom and he didn't like it. Flora said, "Oh my God, you *are* spying on me," and Dad said that's what happens when you let your parents friend you on Facebook.

"I don't believe this!" Flora cried.

"I don't like boyfriends," Dad said. "They disturb things."

"Like kittens?" Mum said. They looked at each other and once again I got the feeling that they were talking about something else completely.

"Ignore your father," Mum said. "He's just trying to provoke you."

"No I'm not," Dad said. "I am trying to *protect* her."

"That fight was completely out of character," Flora insisted. "He was upset."

Mum said she was absolutely certain Zach was a very nice boy, and she hoped he would come to the house one day so she could meet him. Flora said that would probably scare him off for good.

"He's not used to this sort of thing." She waved at Mum and Jas and me, all piled on the bed, with Dad lounging in a chair with his feet up on the bedside table.

"I don't think your mother was planning on receiving him in her *bedroom*," Dad said, and Flora swept out, saying he was impossible, and pretending not to notice that everyone was laughing at her.

"How is Jake?" Mum asked me to change the subject.

"Forget about Jake!" Flora cried from the landing. "They haven't even *kissed* yet!"

"I'm glad to hear it!" Dad roared back at her.

If you could die from blushing, I would be stone-cold dead.

"Actually," I muttered, "I have a date with him this afternoon."

"That's wonderful!" Mum patted my hand. "And you mustn't worry about the kissing." She yawned. "There's plenty of time for that."

And just like that, she fell asleep. Jas and I stared at her, amazed.

"Do you think she's all right?" Jas whispered.

"She looks quite peaceful," I whispered back.

"Plenty of time for kissing," Jas smirked.

"Shut up," I said.

Flora is so right not to want Zach to meet our family.

I couldn't bring myself to write about my date with Jake yesterday. It was sort of—hurtful. I stayed in my room all of Sunday, and thought about not going to school at all today, except unlike Zach's mother Mum doesn't believe in people missing school unless they are ill.

Dodi pounced on me straight after registration, having already heard the most essential details.

"Tom and Colin went too?" she cried. "I don't believe it!"

"How did you know?" I asked.

"Cressida saw you on line. She couldn't believe it either. She says you went to see *X-Men!*"

"I happen to like *X-Men*," I lied. I couldn't tell her the truth, either about the film, or about the fact that Jake hardly talked to me the whole time.

Dodi said that the point wasn't whether I liked it or not, the point was it just wasn't the sort of film you took someone to on a first date, with or without a posse of your best friends.

"I can't believe Cressida is gossiping about me," I said.

"The problem is that you're too familiar," Dodi said. "Jake sees you too much as a friend."

"The problem," I corrected her, "is that he obviously doesn't want to go out with me anymore."

"You have to make yourself more alluring," Dodi decided.

"How?" I asked.

"More seductive."

"HOW?" I repeated.

"Pout, or flutter your eyelashes or something. Maybe giggle when he talks to you. Put on some more lip gloss. I haven't seen you wear makeup once since your makeover."

"Lip gloss makes my lips sticky," I said. "And I refuse to giggle. Flora does it all the time with Zach and it's really annoying."

Dodi rolled her eyes like I was the annoying one.

"Smile," she ordered.

I grinned, baring my teeth.

"Not at me!" she screeched. "At him! And *nicely*! Take off your glasses."

I put my glasses in my pocket and smiled more softly.

"Good," said Dodi. "You know, you really are so pretty when you try. And now I'm going to talk to Jake again."

"I'd really rather you didn't," I told her, but she was already gone.

THE SAGA OF BLUEBELL AND JAKE
THE KISS (TAKE 2)

BLUE, accompanied by DODI, comes out of the school gate. JAKE is waiting on the pavement. Dodi nudges Blue, who removes her glasses. She is wearing lip gloss. Jake leaves TOM and COLIN and marches up to her, looking determined and still a little bit tanned and therefore quite handsome.

> JAKE
> (sounding as determined as he looks)
> Walk you home?

> BLUE
> (beaming, trying not to look like this whole episode isn't mortifying)
> Why thank you, kind sir.

Together, they head off toward the park. Blue steals a glance over her shoulder. Dodi pouts and blows kisses.

Colin and Tom see her and snigger. Jake ignores them. Blue carries on beaming despite aching cheek muscles.

    JAKE
    Shall we sit on this bench?

    BLUE
    That would be lovely.

They stop at a park bench. For a while, they sit side by side in silence. Then Jake turns toward Blue. Blue, still manically grinning, turns toward Jake. Jake clears his throat, leans forward and kisses Blue on the mouth. Blue, resisting the very real urge to giggle, kisses him back. Jake closes his eyes. She closes hers.

FRIDAY, DECEMBER 13

I tried to avoid Jake for most of the week. It was all I wanted to do, after that date. All I could think was if he didn't see me, he wouldn't be able to dump me. Being dumped by Jake would just be the most humiliating thing in the world.

By sliding into lessons at the last minute, eating lunch in the library, and hiding in the girls' bathroom at the end of the day, I managed not to speak to him for days, but there's no escaping Dodi when she's on a mission.

Flora, who heard about the disastrous film date from Cressida's older sister, said I should be the one dumping Jake, not running scared that he was going to dump me. I told her, "If I dump him, it will show he upset me, and that would be embarrassing too," and she said that was stupid but I'm really, really glad now that I didn't listen to her, just like I'm really glad Dodi's my best friend.

The Earth didn't spin the second time Jake kissed me, but it was a lot better.

In fact it was quite nice.

I'm not sure I can write about it right now. I'm feeling a little bit giddy.

SATURDAY, DECEMBER 14

Today I had to take Jas to her riding lesson. This is something Dad normally does, but apparently he has reached another critical point in his novel and cannot be interrupted whatever the circumstances.

Riding lessons were Jas's birthday present from Grandma before she left for Arizona. Grandma, who is horse mad, almost wept when Jas asked for them in the summer. She even rang Jas up from the ranch where she is staying on the first night of her holiday to rant about GALLOPING ON THE WIDE OPEN PLAINS and THE BEAUTY OF SIMPLE HONEST HORSE FOLK and how happy she was that she and Jas might one day be SHARING THIS TOGETHER.

The stables where Jas goes are right beneath the motorway, a tiny yard sandwiched between a bus depot and a leisure center. They are about as far from the wide open plains as it is possible to get, but I can see why Jas loves them. It is rather incredible, after walking from the train down an alleyway covered in graffiti, to stumble on a lot of plump, glossy ponies. Jas skipped into the yard like she owned the place and ran up to greet a young woman who was striding around the yard in skintight jodhpurs and knee-high riding boots, cracking a whip and barking orders at about half a dozen children who were scurrying around with saddles.

"This is Gloria," Jas announced. "Gloria, this is my sister Blue."

"Very pleased to meet you," Gloria said. "You can help Jas tack up Mopsy."

I followed Jas into the tack room, where an old man who looked like a bum sat drinking tea.

"That's Bill," Jas whispered. "He's Gloria's father. He used to be a jockey."

Bill looked like he could barely walk, let alone ride a horse. I waved at him. He grunted. Jas reached behind him to pick up a bridle.

"Not that one," he snapped.

If anyone at home ever spoke to Jas like that, she would probably burst into tears, but here she just laughed, picked up a different bridle, and skipped out again to tack up her pony. The old man watched her go, and I swear I thought he might be smiling, but when he saw me watching he went straight back to being grumpy.

The lesson was a typical riding lesson, lots of girls and one boy following each other nose to tail around the ring, with Gloria shouting instructions at them through a loudspeaker. I watched Jas bounce around an obstacle course. Her pony knocked over two traffic cones and a tub of plastic geraniums. Gloria made her do it again. Crouched over the pony's neck, her black hair falling about her face and her cheeks flushed, Jas was like a different person, happy and confident, like she could take on anything. It was strange, looking at her. It made me wonder if this was the real Jas, as she was meant to be, as opposed to the Jas we see every day, who cries and worries and gets cross. It felt almost like I didn't know her. And then that made me think about how well we know anybody, including ourselves.

Jake's family have friends over from Australia this weekend, which means I can't see him. I asked him if he couldn't sneak away, just for a little bit, but he said no and he would see me at school on Monday.

Monday feels like an awfully long way away. I think I do like Jake now.

I can't believe I have a proper boyfriend! Mum came into my room tonight after I had gone to bed. She hasn't done that for ages. I thought, maybe mothers have a sort of instinct about these things and she has come to talk to me about Jake, but she didn't say anything at all for a really long time. She didn't get into bed with me, either, like she used to, but instead sat on my window seat, looking out at the garden even though it was completely dark.

"We'll have to get a Christmas tree soon," she said at last.

I got a lump in my throat then, because I thought I knew then what was troubling her. Christmas trees are always difficult in our family, because they always remind us of Iris.

"It'll be okay," I said.

"Will it?" she asked. She looked like she often looks these days, like she's about to cry, and I finally screwed up the courage to ask what I haven't asked since she had that secret appointment with the doctor.

"Mum, are you sure you're okay?" I asked.

"What do you mean?"

"You seem so sad."

"I'm always sad at this time of year."

"Apart from that."

"There is nothing to worry about," Mum said, and I know I should have been nice, but I'm really tired of her secrets. So instead I said that if there was nothing else she needed could she please get out of my room because I wanted to go to sleep.

"Don't be cross," she said.

"Don't be annoying," I replied.

She left, like I asked, but then I wished she hadn't. I'm not quite sure how you do tell your mum about your boyfriend, but I think it might have been nice to talk to her about Jake. And we used to have this thing in our family, before Iris died, where nobody was allowed to go to bed angry or sad, but that clearly doesn't apply anymore.

THE FILM DIARIES OF BLUEBELL GADSBY
SCENE FIVE (TRANSCRIPT)
THE DINNER PARTY

INTERIOR, NIGHT.

Once again, we are in the Gadsby family kitchen, with
MOTHER at the cooking range, this time doing something complicated with prunes. A leg of lamb rests on
top of the stove, and an apple tart sits on the side,
next to a bowl of custard.

FATHER sets the table. Under strict instructions, he
takes unusual care over this, putting out candles and
silverware and the tablecloth inherited from Mother's grandmother, vintage linen with lace trimmings.
JASMINE sits on the sofa with her nose in a book and
the kittens in her lap. Father places plates of smoked
salmon on the table.

FATHER

(irritable)

It would be nice if at least one of my daughters
helped me.

MOTHER

(oddly soothing)

Don't be cross, darling. I asked Blue to film this.
I thought it would be nice. Jas, give your father a
hand.

Jasmine sighs and peels herself off the sofa. The kittens (now over four months old and no longer tiny)
start to pad around the room.

JASMINE

(taking in extent of food spread for the first time)

Is anyone coming for dinner?

MOTHER

(sounding nervous)

No darling, just us. Your father and I . . .

FATHER

(warning)

Cassie!

FLORA

(bursting into the kitchen)

He's here! He's nearly here! Is everything ready?

(she takes in the table, the napkins, the roast
lamb)

What are you doing? He'll be terrified! I said it
would just be pasta!

FATHER

What on earth are you talking about?

FLORA

Zach! I asked him and Zoran for dinner. Mum,
didn't you get my text?

MOTHER

(looking appalled)

My phone's dead.

FATHER

(looking furious)

Call him right now and tell him he can't come!

FLORA

Oh my God, what is *wrong* with you?

TWIG enters in his underpants. Flora screams at him
to put some clothes on. Twig replies that he doesn't
have any clothes because Mother accidentally donated
all his jeans to charity. Mother replies he should stop
complaining about his clothes being too small. Twig
answers that normal people buy replacement clothes
before giving the old ones away. Flora declares there is
no way she is letting her boyfriend see her brother naked. Hermione quietly hops onto the table and starts to
eat the smoked salmon. Father bats her away, knocking
over a bottle of red wine.

MOTHER

My grandmother's tablecloth!

FATHER

(roaring)

TO HELL WITH THE TABLECLOTH! AND TO HELL
WITH CATS AND CANDLES AND INCONVENIENT
BOYFRIENDS! TO HELL WITH ALL THE THINGS
CONSTANTLY CONSPIRING TO DISRUPT
EVERYTHING I TRY TO DO!

The whole family stares at him, fascinated. Nobody but
CAMERAMAN notices the kitchen door open, revealing
a worried-looking Zoran and a frankly petrified-looking
Zach.

MOTHER

David, calm down.

FATHER

THIS IS NOT WHAT THIS EVENING WAS MEANT
TO BE ABOUT!

ZORAN

(very softly)

What was it meant to be about, David?

Father slumps, looking defeated and almost as terrified as Zach. Mother goes to him, takes his hand, then turns to face the camera.

    MOTHER
    We're going to have a baby.

SUNDAY, DECEMBER 15

Poor Zach. I bet he thought the first time he met Flora's family it would be all about him. He probably rehearsed it in front of the mirror in Zoran's tiny bathroom, wondering if he should call Dad *sir* or *Mr. Gadsby*, and was it all right to wear a hoodie or should he wear a shirt and should he buy Mum flowers or stuff like that. I bet he had no idea he was going to stumble into a room full of flying kittens and a load of people screaming and crying because they'd just heard life-changing news, straight after hearing himself described as *inconvenient*. I bet that was the last thing he expected.

"This is not unusual behavior," I heard Zoran reassure Zach as they stood in the doorway, and then he was sweeping into the room and hugging Mum.

"You told them at last!" he said.

"You knew!" I cried.

"I've been begging him to come back when the baby is born," Mum sniffed. "And I was so worried how you all would take the news, with the age difference and everything."

I knew that by *everything*, she meant Iris. Apparently Zoran has been saying she should tell us for ages but she was too scared. Then when I got cross with her last night she realized she couldn't keep it secret anymore.

"Are you happy?" she asked me.

"I think so," I stammered.

"A baby!" Flora looked stunned.

"Will it be a boy?" Twig asked.

Jas didn't say anything to Mum or Dad at all. Instead she moved away from the little crowd gathered around the parents, making a beeline for Zach, looking very shy but also quite determined.

"I loved your song," I heard her whisper to him. Zach stopped looking scared and looked embarrassed instead.

"Can I ask you a question?" she asked, and then she saw me listening and frowned for me to go away.

Dinner was nice and barely burned at all. I think Mum was so relieved her secret was finally out she couldn't stop laughing. She actually thought she couldn't have babies anymore, so it took her ages to realize she was pregnant. She's known for months, but she and Dad didn't want to tell us until they were used to the idea.

"We were a bit shaken up at first," Mum said.

I'm not sure Dad is at all used to the idea of the baby yet. When Flora asked if they had thought of any names yet, and Mum said what did we think about Hazel, either for a boy or a girl, he winced, and not just because he doesn't like the name Hazel. Talking about names, he said, made the whole thing feel more real.

"Of course it's real!" Flora cried. "Now I know Mum's pregnant, I can see the bump and everything! I can't believe we didn't notice before!"

"It will be all right, David." Mum beamed, and Dad gulped down more wine.

Twig, Jas, and I didn't say much at all, but Flora and Zoran made up for it. Some people are like that, they can just chat away nonstop whatever is going on, as if a massive bombshell hasn't just landed on them. Zach sat next to Flora, and at first he was completely silent, but then Mum asked him how his grandfather was and about his music, and Dad started going on about how he was in a band at school and reminiscing about all the gigs he used to go to, and Flora looked like she might die of embarrassment except it turns out that Zach likes a lot of the music Dad used to like. And then Twig, who was sitting on the other side of him, started to talk to him about football, and also asked him if he was any good at carpentry, because would he like to finish building the tree house, and even though Zach didn't become exactly talkative, he stopped looking like the whole plan for the evening was to flay him alive and throw his body to a pack of ravenous vultures.

I didn't talk to him until the end of the evening, because I was building up the courage for what I had to say. But just before they left, when Zoran was hugging everyone and Zach was standing on his own, I went up to him and apologized. I didn't even try to blame it on Dodi. I'd actually rehearsed a whole speech, but in the end all I managed to mumble was, "I'm really sorry about the video," and he blushed and mumbled back, "Hey, don't worry about it." I thought we were going to leave it at that but then he added, "Actually, I looked at it again, and it's pretty funny," and suddenly I completely got why Flora is so crazy about him. I know it's a cliché, but his whole face really does light up when he smiles, and he has this way of looking at you, like you really matter.

Zach is lovely.

The parents think so too. "What a nice boy," Mum said when they had gone. Dad said yes, and did she think he should take up the guitar again, and then they went up to bed hand in hand like they'd never had a fight in their whole lives. And Flora beamed and floated on upstairs after them, followed by Twig who is pleased because in one evening he has accumulated not only a sort of brother-in-law who plays football and can build tree houses, but also potentially an actual brother.

Which just left Jas and me.

A *baby*.

I can't believe it.

MONDAY, DECEMBER 16

A baby. Not a fatal illness or imminent death or divorce. A *baby*.

On the way to school this morning, Flora said, "You do realize what this means, don't you, it means the parents still do it." Jas said, "Do what?" and Flora said, "Well how do you think babies are made?" Twig made a gagging noise. Jas blushed scarlet and said, "Oh that, I know that!" and then we were silent, all thinking private thoughts about Mum and Dad making babies. It was an enormous relief when Dodi bounced up to us at the crossroads.

"What's up?" Dodi asked. "You all look a bit sick."

I told her, and then immediately felt guilty because I'm

sure her reaction was exactly what mine should have been.

"That's AMAZING!" Dodi shouted. "A baby! I love babies! They're so cute!"

"They cry all night and they poo in their pants," said Twig. "How is that cute?"

"Oh my God!" Dodi was struck by a sudden thought and just looking at her I could tell what it was. "That means your parents still . . ."

I felt better.

"Babies *are* cute." Flora brightened. "When it's born, Zach and I can take it to the park and pretend it's ours!"

Twig said that was just weird, but I wish I could be like Flora. Life must be so simple when you're her.

Me and Dodi skipped assembly. Dodi pretended to have really bad cramps and I said I had to look after her, and we settled on the floor of the science block toilets, which are still pretty clean first thing in the morning.

"Are you pleased?" Dodi asked, and I told her I didn't know.

"I bet it's weird," she said, and I said yes, it was.

"But still, nice," said Dodi. "And you mustn't think about Iris. It's not about her, it's not about her at all."

That is why, however annoying she can be, I love Dodi. Because she always knows what I'm thinking.

I wanted to talk to Jake about the baby too, but he was

really quiet today. "That's so awesome," he said when I told him, but then when I tried to explain how I was feeling about it, I could tell he wasn't really listening.

"Boys are rubbish at emotional stuff," Dodi said to make me feel better.

"Jake never used to be," I replied. Dodi said that she had read in a magazine that some boys find it quite hard to go from friend to boyfriend, and that I had to try and be understanding and give him time and space. So when Jake told me he couldn't walk home with me after school this afternoon, I just smiled like I really couldn't care less and said that was fine, because I couldn't walk home with him, either, and then I went to meet Mum at her office.

I waited for her outside. She came out looking tired but sort of smiley, and like Flora I wondered how none of us never even noticed how much she's changed. Now that I know she's pregnant, it seems so obvious. It's not so much that she has a big round tummy, but her whole body is so much *thicker* than it used to be. Zoran once told me that people only ever see what they want to see, and I suppose he must be right.

"Blue!" She jumped when she saw me, but I don't think she was that surprised. I said could we talk, and she tucked her arm into mine and said she knew just the place.

The church was small and dark and cold, but it smelled

of incense and someone had put flowers in front of the altar. A priest in long dark robes was talking to an old lady in one of the front pews. He raised his hand at Mum and smiled like he knew her.

"I come in here sometimes at lunchtime," Mum said. "It's a nice place to be quiet."

She led me to one of those tables where you can light candles and put some coins in the box.

"It's not Christmas yet," I said.

Christmas is pretty much the only time we ever go to church, to remember Iris, who died on Christmas Eve.

Mum just handed me a candle. I tried to pray, but I'm not very good at praying, so I thought instead. I thought about how Iris would feel if it was her standing here instead of me. Iris loved baby animals, and really a human baby isn't so different from, say, a puppy or a kitten. I thought about how she would never know this baby, and how wrong that was.

"Do you want to feel it kicking?" Mum whispered, and I wasn't sure, but she took my hand anyway and put it against her tummy underneath her coat. Apparently I used to always feel Twig and Jas kick when she was pregnant with them, but I can't remember it and I wasn't expecting it to feel like that, so *strong*. I jumped when the baby kicked my hand, and screamed out loud. The priest and the old lady looked up, saw what was going on and smiled.

"How do you think it feels for *me*?" Mum laughed.

"Do you already love it?" I asked. "Like you love us?"

She took so long to answer I thought maybe she wasn't going to, but then she said that the way you love a baby is very different from the way you love an older child and that sometimes she thought she loved us all more and more as we grew up. She said nothing mattered more to her in the whole world than keeping us safe and that it still destroyed her to know she couldn't stop bad things happening to us, and did I understand?

I nodded. I couldn't speak, because I had such a big lump in my throat.

"You mustn't worry if you don't know what to make of it. It's a lot to think about. Babies upset things, as your father might say."

"Like boyfriends," I said. "And kittens."

I reached out to touch her tummy again. It felt different this time, bigger and rounder than the sharp limb which had jabbed at me earlier

"The head," Mum said.

"Will I hurt it?"

"It's tougher than you think."

I don't know how long we sat there, me with my head on Mum's shoulder, her arms around me and my hand on the baby's head in her tummy. Eventually the old priest coughed and said he was sorry to disturb us but he had to close the church. Mum squeezed me tight before letting me go.

"I want us to make this the best Christmas," she said. She didn't say, "since Iris died," but I knew what she meant. She never answered my question about loving the baby, but she didn't need to.

WEDNESDAY, DECEMBER 18

We broke up for the holidays at lunchtime. I went to Home Sweet Home with the others. Colin, Dodi, and Tom were messing around, trying to remember all the verses of "Rudolph the Red-Nosed Reindeer." I sat next to Jake, who was still being really quiet, and then when we left the café I hung back so I could walk with him and asked if he was okay.

Jake said that he was fine.

"You know you can talk to me about anything, right?" I said.

The others had all stopped at the little Christmas market which has been up since the beginning of December. Mostly they sell things like food and mulled wine and expensive stuff we can't afford, but one stall has an everything under £2.99 section, including a Santa badge Colin was buying for his little sister.

"It's so awesome," he said. "Look what happens when you press the middle."

We looked. The badge lit up and started playing "Jingle Bells." We all laughed, even Jake.

He has a nice laugh.

"That's amazing," I said, because it kind of was.

"My sister's going to love it," Colin said.

"What are you getting Blue for Christmas, Jake?" Dodi asked.

Jake looked a bit panicked at that and said he hadn't thought about it. I said it didn't matter, I hadn't bought him anything yet either, and I was going shopping for presents on Saturday.

"But Jake's going to his gran's tomorrow," Tom said. "You'd better get him something before he goes, Blue, or he might dump you."

Dodi told Tom he was an idiot.

"I thought you weren't going to your gran's till Christmas Eve?" I said to Jake, and he went very red and said that things had changed and he was going early.

A band started playing Christmas songs, and Dodi dragged me off to look at them. The boys joined us a few minutes later. Jake was quieter than ever on the way home, but when we said good-bye in the park, he gave me my present, which was a Santa badge.

"I bought it when you were listening to the band," he said, looking embarrassed. "You said Colin's was amazing."

I pressed the middle. My badge doesn't play "Jingle Bells," but Santa still lights up, and he goes *Ho, Ho, Ho* instead.

"I love it," I said, and kissed him on the cheek.

There was an enormous Christmas tree standing in the hall when I got home, and Flora, Twig, and Jas were all sitting on the stairs as Zach and Dad struggled to get it straight. Zach is basically at our house all the time now. I think he's been here every single day after school. Twig has got him working on the tree house and Jas keeps dragging him off for secret talks (which really annoys Flora), and Mum has asked him to stay for supper twice. She's even invited him to come for Christmas.

I don't care what Dodi says about boys needing time and space. I just sent Jake a picture of all of us, including Zach decorating the tree. "Wish you were here too!" I wrote, because it was true. Then I told him I was wearing his badge and added lots of kisses.

Dodi is going skiing with her parents for Christmas this year, but before she left we spent the whole morning at Portobello Market rummaging through secondhand bookstalls until I found exactly what I wanted for Jake, two almost-perfect early 1980s *X-Men* comics.

"Nice," Zach said when I showed them to him. "How much did you pay?"

I told him. Then when he looked shocked I said I could have paid a load more, but the person who sold them to me gave me a good price because one of them is a bit torn. Zach, who is kind, said they were a really cool present and Jake would be thrilled. Flora, who is not kind, told me later that Zach said I'd been completely cheated. She said 1980s comics weren't valuable at all, and next time I should ask Zach for his advice, because he knew all about it.

"I can't believe Jake buys you a singing badge and you spend all that money on *X-Men* comics," Flora said.

"It's not about the money," I said, and then I texted Jake to tell him I've got him the best present ever.

He wrote, *You shouldn't have, I only got you that badge.*

I wrote, *I love that badge,* and he sent me a smiley face.

It made me feel all warm inside.

WEDNESDAY, DECEMBER 25

It has been a good Christmas.

Yesterday was Iris's death day. We went to church again, all six of us, not to a service or anything, just us, like the other day with Mum.

"Everything is changing," I told Iris in church yesterday. "Mum and Dad are having a baby; Twig and Jas are growing up; Flora has this boyfriend who is practically living with us; and I'm going out with Jake. Remember Jake, from primary school? I really like him. Flora loves change, but I don't, not really. I was just getting used to the way things were, you know? I don't know if I'm ready for a whole new set of things." Dad was praying next to me, his lips moving and everything, and since I know he doesn't believe in God, I knew that he was talking to Iris too. He saw me looking at him and held out his hand.

"Do you think she minds about the baby?" he asked.

"I think she's sad she won't be here for it, but I don't think she minds," I told him.

Dad blinked very fast so I wouldn't notice he was crying.

"Don't be scared," I whispered.

"I'm not scared," he whispered back.

"Me neither." I smiled, and he smiled back.

"I'm ****** petrified," he admitted.

Zach didn't come for Christmas Day, despite Mum's invitation. He really wanted to, but Zoran says that family is family, and took him to visit his grandfather in hospital in the country, and they're stopping at the Richmond Hill Retirement Home on the way back to visit Zoran's great-aunt Alina. Flora says Zach was really hoping his mum would come for Christmas, but he still hasn't heard from her.

We are going to Zoran's for lunch tomorrow, but yesterday and today were just about us. It was a completely uneventful day. Just the six of us, shuffling about in our pajamas, opening presents, and eating cake for breakfast and going for a walk because Mum said we had to. Flora cooked dinner. She says she needs the practice for when she leaves home to go and live in a flat with lots of other actors, probably in New York or Los Angeles or somewhere. This basically meant that all of us except Mum (who was resting) and Dad (who was writing—apparently holidays don't count if you are a creative genius) spent most of the afternoon in the kitchen, which ended up looking even worse than when Mum cooks.

After all our hard work, the turkey was tough, the vegetables weren't properly cooked, and the potatoes completely burned because Flora decided to do a one-woman rendition of *A Christmas Carol* when she was meant to be lightly parboiling them. But Jas decorated the table with

Christmas themed Haribos; Twig made rum and raisin reindeer-shaped cookies; I made gravy out of a packet which made everything taste nice, if not delicious; and Dad drank too much port as usual and fell asleep on the sofa with Mum while we were cleaning up.

"Look!" Jas dragged us over to look at them. Mum lay at one end of the sofa with her head thrown back and her mouth open, snoring lightly, both hands on her tummy. Dad lay at the other end, his head turned into the cushions, snoring much more loudly, completely unaware of Ron and Hermione, also sleeping and snoring, stretched out across his lap.

Absolutely nothing happened this Christmas, but Mum got what she wanted: It was the best one since Iris died.

THE FILM DIARIES OF BLUEBELL GADSBY
SCENE SIX (TRANSCRIPT)
BOXING DAY LUNCH

INTERIOR, DAY

Inside Zoran's flat. The small table by the window is
crowded with chairs and the remains of lunch (cas-
serole of pork with apricots, shredded greens with
chestnuts, cheese and herb dumplings, trifle). ZORAN,
JAS, and TWIG sit cross-legged on the floor in front of
the coffee table, eating a huge tin of traditional Bos-
nian biscuits known as bear paws, made with walnuts
and tossed in sugar (a present from Alina). MOTHER
and ZACH sit on the sofa, watching FLORA, who stands
before them, trying to act out *Pirates of the Caribbean:
Dead Man's Chest* while CAMERAMAN (Blue) films.

They are playing charades.

Jas, Twig, and Cameraman knew the title the moment Flora started to act it out, but Mother and Zach haven't got a clue.

> MOTHER
> *Harry Potter!*

> ZACH
> *Batman!*

> MOTHER
> *Dracula! Robin Hood! Les Misérables!*

The doorbell rings. Zoran pads over to the intercom to buzz open the door to the street, then flings open the door to the flat and stands straight like a soldier, holding out the biscuit tin. Nobody else pays attention. They are expecting Father, who skipped lunch to work on his book.

> ZACH
> *Pirates of the Caribbean!*

Flora squeals and jumps up and down, making wild hand gestures.

ZACH

Curse of the Black Pearl! At World's End!! On Stranger Tides!!!

FLORA

YOU ARE BOTH COMPLETELY USELESS!

MOTHER

I know, I know! *Dead Man's Chest!!!!!*

FLORA

FINALLY!

By now, Mother and Zach are crying with laughter and hugging each other. Flora drops down next to them, telling them again they were useless. Mother hugs her too.

Zoran comes in from the hallway. Alone.

ZORAN

(very serious)

Zach, you have a visitor.

Zach looks up, still laughing, from the sofa, where Twig and Jas have joined them. A woman walks into the room behind Zoran. Tall, pale, with purple smudges under her dark eyes and long black hair, wrapped in a pale gray cashmere coat which she hugs to her body as if, despite the weather, she is cold. She looks like a fairy-tale queen, or maybe a witch. She also looks familiar.

Mother, Flora, Jas, and Twig, sensing something is wrong, move away from Zach, who scrambles up from the sofa to stand before the stranger.

    ZACH
    Mum!

Mother signals to Cameraman to stop filming.

Camera goes black.

THURSDAY, DECEMBER 26

Zach stared like he couldn't believe his eyes.

"Surprise!" she said, but she sounded nervous.

Zach opened his mouth, but no sound came out. Her face fell. He took a step toward her and held out his hand,

112

but it was shaking. He let it drop like he didn't know what to do with it.

Mum pushed herself up and came to stand beside him, putting her own hand out to steady his.

"We're very pleased to meet you," she said. "We're all so fond of Zach."

Zach's mother looked around the room, took in Jas and Twig on the sofa, Zoran, Flora, me, before coming back to let her eyes rest on Zach.

"Won't you sit down?"

Zoran gestured toward the sofa. Twig and Jas jumped off it. Flora also came to stand beside Zach and took his other hand. His mother sat down, still wearing her coat.

"Say something, Zach," Flora whispered, but he still couldn't speak.

"This was a mistake." Zach's mother was already back on her feet. "I have to go," she said, and hurried out of the room. Zach came back to life, shouted "Mum!" and ran after her. After a moment's hesitation, Zoran followed.

"No," Mum said as Flora started to go after Zoran, and then she cried, "Twig, stop that, it's dangerous!" because he was leaning right out of the window, looking into the street.

"You can see really well from here," he said, and we all leaned out, ignoring Mum.

Down on the pavement, Zach's mother was trying to get into a car, but Zach stood in her way. She pushed him, jumped into the car, and drove away.

Even four stories up, we heard Zach shout, "Mum!"

He ran after her but she didn't stop. He went halfway down the street and then gave up.

Flora ran downstairs, but Zoran got there. He pulled Zach out of the road and then he just stood there, with his arms around him, holding him and holding him while Zach cried like I've never seen a boy cry in my entire life.

FRIDAY, DECEMBER 27

Flora says she was right all along and that Zach's mother is a witch. She went to see Zach this morning, and came into my room when she got back to tell me about it. I knew the minute she came in that she was in a really bad mood.

"I don't care how nice she ever was to him," she said. "All that going to the seaside and tea at the Ritz. She's horrible and I hate her."

"What happened?"

She flopped down on my bed and closed her eyes. "We quarreled," she sighed.

This is how it happened. When Flora arrived at Zoran's

flat, he said that Zach had gone to the park with his basket-ball, so she followed him there.

"He was all alone on the court," she said. "Just like the first time I spoke to him."

She watched him play until he stopped, and then she called out to him. Normally, she says, his whole face lights up when he sees her, but today he just said, "Oh it's you," and that's when they had their first argument, right there on the basketball court. Flora said, "Aren't you going to kiss me hello," and Zach said, "What's the point," and Flora wasn't quite sure what to answer to that so she said, "I'm so sorry about your mum," and Zach said, "Yah, well," and they sat down on a bench, and Flora said, "I can't believe she could be so horrible." Zach said, "It's not like that," and Flora said, "Well what is it like then," and suddenly they were shouting at each other, all about Zach's mum and how Flora with her ******* perfect family could never understand what it was like for him.

"I said don't talk about my family like that, and then we yelled some more, and he left."

"He really said that about us?" I asked.

Flora said, "Yes, he did."

"But we're not perfect," I said. "We're so very far from perfect."

"That's not all," Flora said. She was huddled up in a ball

on my bed, with a blanket wrapped around her, and for the first time I realized that she looked scared as well as angry. "I think she was there, Blue," she said.

"What do you mean?"

"Zach's mother. He stormed off and didn't see her, but I did. Standing at the edge of the court, you know where the big trees are? She must have been hiding there the whole time."

"Are you sure it was her?"

"I didn't see her face," Flora admitted. "And she was wearing a hat, but it was the same coat, and she *was* watching us. It was creepy, Blue."

"We should tell the parents," I said.

"Tell them what?" Flora asked. "They'll only go and talk to Zoran, and then Zach will be even more furious with me." And then she repeated how much she hated Zach's stupid mother, and stormed off to talk to Tamsin.

Zoran spoke to Mr. Rudowski yesterday to tell him what had happened, and also to ask him to explain Zach's mother's behavior, but Mr. Rudowski was so upset that one of the nurses took the telephone away from him and told Zoran to let him be. I overheard Zoran tell Mum when he came around this evening to bring back a bag she forgot at his flat. He's spoken to Alina about it too. Alina says she doesn't know any details, but that Wanda (Zach's mother) had always been what she calls *problematic* and had a *history of mental illness.*

Zoran is taking Zach away. Alina has a friend with a little cottage by the sea near Brighton, and he has agreed to lend it to Zoran. "It will do us both good to get away for a while," Zoran said.

Flora says, "Good riddance," and she never wants to see Zach again, but I know she doesn't mean it. She keeps checking her phone for messages from him. And Jas is upset as well. She just came into my room too, as I was writing this, and asked did I know when Zach was coming back.

I said that I had no idea, and she crept out again, looking dejected.

SATURDAY, DECEMBER 28

Grandma has arrived, on her way back to Devon from Arizona. Dad went to fetch her at the airport, and she is going to stay for a week, while Dad whisks Mum away to Paris for a few days of Being Romantic.

Having Grandma here has cheered everybody up. Grandma can be maddening, and she is even more bossy than Flora, but it's difficult to be miserable when she's around. For one thing, she is one of the loudest people I know. She landed at six o'clock this morning. By half-past seven she was in our kitchen cooking the most enormous pan of fried eggs I have ever seen, as well as a skyscraper of pancakes.

"AMERICAN BREAKFASTS!" Grandma bellowed, pouring maple syrup over everything. "ABSOLUTELY MARVELOUS! NO NEED TO EAT ANYTHING ELSE FOR THE REST OF THE DAY!"

Grandma has her own view about the baby. "AT YOUR AGE?" she cried when they told her. "ARE YOU MAD?"

"I'm only forty-two," Mum said, and Grandma sniffed and said forty-two should be old enough to see sense but she supposed there was no stopping some people. I could see Mum really wanted to storm out of the kitchen but also that she was torn because everything tastes so delicious when it is covered in maple syrup.

"How are you all taking the news?" Grandma asked more quietly, when I went up to her room to watch her unpack.

"It was a bit of a shock at first." I thought it was probably best not to mention Iris or Dad being scared. Grandma can be very understanding and she is one of my favorite people in the whole world, but it's not always easy to talk to her when she's being disapproving. "We're really happy now," I said. "Dad keeps telling Mum's tummy that he loves it. Twig is convinced he's going to get a brother, and Flora wants to play at being a mum with her boyfriend, Zach, or at least she did until they had a fight."

Then I got distracted, because Grandma had pulled a very torn and battered copy of *Jane Eyre* from her case, and I remembered that I'm supposed to read the first three chapters over the holidays but with all the baby excitement and then Zach I had completely forgotten, and not for the first time I thought that there was something a little bit magic about Grandma, who is able to produce exactly what you need, when you need it.

"Ah, the boyfriend," Grandma said. "Your father told me all about him. And what about you? Are you in love yet?"

There's never any use lying to her.

"I'm not sure about being in love," I told her. "But I am going out with my friend Jake."

Grandma said, "Well I hope you've got him on a good short rein."

I said I didn't really know what that meant, and Grandma said it meant she hoped that Jake was being nice to me, and also that I wasn't letting him walk all over me if he wasn't. "I know what you're like, young Bluebell," she said. "You're too forgiving."

I fingered my Santa badge. "He's very nice to me," I said.

Grandma gave me one of her sharp looks.

"Really," I insisted. "He is."

I didn't want to tell her I haven't heard from Jake since he sent me that smiley way before Christmas. For a start I didn't think she'd approve, but also perhaps this is normal. Just because Flora and Zach are permanently joined at the hip (or used to be, anyway) doesn't mean everybody has to be like that. And anyway, how much can you say in a text?

Grandma was still looking at me.

"Some things fit and some just don't," she said. "Not enough people remember that." And then she changed the subject and said why didn't I read *Jane Eyre* out loud to her while she finished unpacking.

I've been reading it all day. "It's a lot better than I thought it would be," I told Grandma this evening at supper, and she smiled and said wasn't it wonderful when life turned out that way.

SUNDAY, DECEMBER 29

Flora is starting to get twitchy about New Year's Eve, and the fact that she still hasn't heard from Zach. She was going to go down to Trafalgar Square with him to see the fireworks, and now she doesn't know what to do.

"Can't you go with Tamsin instead?" I asked, and she said that wasn't the point. She called Zoran to ask him when they were coming back and he said he didn't know. Then she asked him why Zack wasn't answering her texts, and he said he didn't know about that either, but to give him time.

"How much time does he need?" Flora moaned after she'd spoken to Zoran. "I've said I'm sorry about a million times, even though he hasn't once apologized to me. Just because he's so worked up about his crazy mother, why does that mean he can't talk to me?"

Grandma said boys often find it difficult to think about more than one thing at once.

"He'd better come back soon," said Twig. "Or we'll never finish the tree house."

"I really, really need to speak to him," whispered Jas. "Can I have his phone number?"

Flora shouted, "For God's sake, no wonder he doesn't want to see me anymore!" and you could tell she was going to cry because her nose was blotchy. "The way you go on," she screamed, "you've probably scared him off!" And then she ran upstairs, and sure enough she hadn't even reached the landing before she burst into noisy sobs.

That was this morning. Then Dodi rang to say she was back and what was *I* doing for New Year's.

"Are you seeing Jake?" she asked. "Shall we all do something together?"

I said Jake was still at his grandparents', and Dodi said, "No, he's back." And then her voice went a bit funny and she said, "Didn't you know that?" and even though we were on the phone I blushed, and said no I didn't but it didn't matter.

"He's been back since Boxing Day," Dodi said. "I spoke to Colin last night. I can't believe he hasn't called you."

"We're not really like that," I said, but I couldn't really believe it either.

"You're his *girlfriend*," Dodi said. "What you need to do is call him up *right now* to tell him he can't treat you like that. On second thought, don't do that, it makes you sound a bit desperate. *I'll* call him."

I held the phone away from my ear and looked at it. Dodi carried on talking. I don't think she even noticed I wasn't listening.

"I never even wanted to go out with Jake in the first place," I told her.

"Well, why did you then?" she asked.

"Because you told me to. You're always telling me what to do."

"Only because you can never decide anything for yourself."

I hung up on her. She called right back, but I ignored her.

It seems quite astonishing to me that Flora and I both have boyfriends who are ignoring us, but at least Zach has the excuse of his mad mother. Jake's just being rude.

I read a load more of *Jane Eyre* today, and what I think is this: if Jane Eyre, who was a weed, could stand up to Mr. Rochester, who was rich and powerful, at a time when women were supposed to be meek and never complain, then I can stand up to Jake and ask him what is going on.

THE SAGA OF BLUEBELL AND JAKE
HEARTBREAKS AND MILK SHAKES

DAY, EXTERIOR, ABOUT THREE O'CLOCK IN THE AF-
TERNOON.

BLUE, carefully attired in a black skinny jeans (her
own), a silvery sequin jumper (borrowed from Dodi
long ago and worn under her orders), duffle coat, her
Santa badge, and one of Flora's hats, shelters at a bus
stop in front of Jake's house, waiting for him to come
out.

The front door opens. Jake emerges. Blue breaks into a
discreet run and catches up with him.

> BLUE
> (masterful, though inwardly quaking)
> Let's go for a coffee?

JAKE

(looking terrified)

Er.

BLUE

(still displaying a strength she does not feel)

Excellent. Let's go to Home Sweet Home.

Cut to interior, Home Sweet Home. Blue and Jake sit at a table by the window. She (being sophisticated) has a cappuccino. He has ordered a chocolate milk shake.

BLUE

(presenting a gift-wrapped package)

This is your Christmas present. It took me ages to find it. I hope you like it.

JAKE

(not looking at her, mumbling so hard he is virtually incomprehensible)

I can't go out with you anymore.

BLUE

(plowing on)

I bought it because I know you love the *X-Men*
films and it reminded me of when we went to the
cinema. You know, with Colin and Tom.

JAKE

(as above)

When I was in Australia at my auntie's wedding
I met my cousin's best friend Talullah and fell in
love with her. I felt really bad because of you, and
so I tried to forget about her and make it work
with you, but then I found out she was coming
over for the holidays. They were the Australian
friends who came to stay with us before
Christmas. After us, they went to stay with Gran.
That's why I left London early, to go and see her.
She has gone back to Australia now, but I still
love her and I don't want to lie to you anymore.
I'm sorry.

BLUE

(shakily)

I can't believe you didn't tell me before.

JAKE

I didn't mean for it to happen. As soon as we
arrived in Melbourne we drove out to the beach to
look at the penguins and Talullah was there. Ever
since I've been very confused.

BLUE

I love penguins.

JAKE

So does Talullah.

BLUE

I suppose I'd better go then.
(hesitates)
You can keep the present.

She rises slowly and walks away feeling crushed and
humiliated. At the door, she turns one last time with
tears in her eyes. Jake is already talking on his phone.
Blue, feeling like she is in a real movie, strides back
across the café to the table where Jake sits.

BLUE

Are you talking to her?

JAKE

What? No! Of course not, it's nighttime in
Australia!

Blue carefully takes back the comics. She removes the
badge and puts it down where the comics were. And
then she picks up Jake's milk shake and empties it
over his head.

MONDAY, DECEMBER 30

I forgot I was cross with Dodi. The first thing I did when I
left the café was call her to tell her what I'd done.

"His milk shake?" Dodi repeated. "All over his head?
Oh, I'm so proud of you!"

I've never heard her laugh so hard at anything.

I think it's the most outrageous thing I have ever done in
my entire life. In fact, I think it may be the *only* outrageous
thing I've ever done, and it felt fantastic. I ran almost the
whole way home. It was raining really hard and I didn't
have an umbrella, but I didn't care. It could have been hail-
ing golf balls and I wouldn't have noticed.

My mood changed as I got wetter and colder. I passed
the cemetery where Jas found the kittens and went in. I

found Violet Buttercream's grave and Jas was right, it is a nice place to sit. "I should be crying," I told myself. The rain fell harder and the light grew dimmer. I was freezing by now. I thought really hard about how my heart had been broken into a thousand tiny pieces, but still the tears didn't come, because what I mainly felt was angry.

All that time wasted thinking about Jake when he wasn't ever thinking about me. He used to be my *friend*. He should never have lied to me.

Jas was sitting at the kitchen table doing homework when I got in. I put the kettle on for tea, then sank onto the sofa and sighed.

In the proper film of my life, this would have been the moment when they play soulful music with a close-up of me gazing moodily out of the window looking brave. The moment when everything is about to change. An *important* moment.

Jas didn't even look up from her books.

"Jake and I have split up," I told her.

Jas sighed, gathered up her papers, and stomped upstairs.

I followed her. On the landing outside our bedrooms, Grandma was lecturing Twig on the rules of football indoors.

"The ball should *not* be muddy," Grandma scolded.

"But I *like* mud," Twig replied.

"I've split up with Jake," I said, but neither of them replied because at that moment Flora stole the limelight as usual, and started screaming on the phone downstairs.

"I don't care about my exams!" Flora shouted. "I want to be an actress and get as far away from my life as possible!"

We all crept down to see what was going on. She was standing in the hall, dripping water everywhere because she doesn't have an umbrella either, yelling at Mum on her phone because she just learned that she got the part she auditioned for weeks ago, but Mum won't let her do it because the play opens right in the middle of Flora's exams.

"WELL I DON'T EXACTLY APPROVE OF YOU HAVING A BABY!" Flora was yelling, which is when Grandma took her phone.

"I'LL TAKE CARE OF THIS END, CASSIE!" Grandma shouts even louder than normal when she's on the phone. "THE MOST IMPORTANT THING RIGHT NOW IS FOR YOU TO STAY CALM!"

After she had hung up, Grandma gave us all a lecture. With Mum in the state she's in, Grandma says, we must be model children. "That means NO SHOUTING," she said. "No mud, no stomping, no moping over boyfriends."

"Actually," I said, "I am not moping over him. If anyone ever listened to me . . ."

"And no interrupting," said Grandma, and told us all to go away while she gave some serious thought to what she was going to do with us because it was obvious we all needed a distraction.

I went down to find her in her room when the others had all gone to bed, and told her about Jake and the milk shake. Her reaction was almost exactly the same as Dodi's. She said it was the funniest thing she'd ever heard and she had never been more proud of me. Then she said that Jake was a snake, a rat, and a scoundrel, and asked me if I was very upset.

I thought about my answer very carefully. "I *am* upset," I said. "But not as much as I think I should be. Mainly I just feel really, really stupid."

Grandma said Jake was the one who was stupid, preferring anyone to her granddaughter, and then she started to chuckle and said, "Oh to have been a fly on the wall at the Home Sweet Home when you threw the milk shake." I just heard her go into the bathroom, and she was still laughing.

Going out with someone because you feel a bit sorry for them is a *really bad idea*. Next year is going to be different, I've decided. Next year I am only going to do things I actually want to do.

WHOLESOME EXERCISE is what Grandma has decided to do with us, and so today she marched us all over to Jas's stables for a riding lesson.

We found Gloria huddled over a gas fire in the tack room going through a wad of papers with a calculator on her knee.

"Bills," Flora whispered. "Red ones."

Gloria sighed when she saw us and explained that if we were good enough she would take us for a ride on the common, but that for our first day we had to pass a test to make sure it was safe and the first thing we should do was tack up the horses. She showed us which ponies we were riding, and then the phone rang and she marched back to the tack room and left us with water dripping down our necks, because obviously it was still raining, clutching saddles and reins and wondering which bits went where.

"You heard her," Grandma said. "Get on with it."

"I have no idea what to do," Twig said.

"You are here to learn," Grandma said.

"I know what to do," Jas said.

"This is a terrible place," Flora announced.

"It's a community project," Grandma corrected her. "It was set up to help children in need."

"Are we children in need?" asked Twig.

"I am," Flora grumbled under her breath. "In need of dry clothes, a boyfriend who calls me back, and a grandmother who isn't insane."

As far as the riding went, we were all hopeless except Jas. The only lessons we have ever had before have been with Grandma and boil down to GO FASTER AND DON'T FALL OFF, but Gloria has a different approach. She made us practice all sorts of exercises like figure eight and changing reins and other stuff none of us understood, first walking, then trotting, until our legs ached and our brains were completely confused.

"I thought that was quite fascinating," Grandma said, when the lesson was over.

"I'm afraid I can't come back," Flora told Gloria firmly. "I'm doing my finals in the summer and I have to study really, really hard."

Twig, who fell off more times than anybody else, said that now he was playing on a team he really had to focus on his football. I wanted to say I couldn't come either, because I have decided that I really, *really* don't like horses, but I didn't want to disappoint Grandma, and also I remembered the calculator and the papers and the way Gloria sighed when we arrived. So instead I said I would love to come back next weekend with Jas and join her regular lesson.

Flora checked her phone again on the way home, but there were still no messages from Zach.

"Do you think he's had an accident?" Jas asked.

"Maybe he fell under a train." Twig was on my laptop looking at train timetables online. I know for a fact he finds trains really, really boring, but Maisie has asked him to babysit her little brother again on Monday after school starts, and Twig is determined to impress the kid with his extensive knowledge. Dodi, who is fascinated by Twig's love life, says surely he must realize how Maisie is using him, but Twig swears she's not like that.

"Maybe he was standing on a railway bridge," Twig said now, "and it was raining, and he leaned over a bit too much and slipped under the four twenty-three from Paddington."

"Could that happen?" Jas looked horrified.

"I think it's quite unlikely," I said. "And I'm sure Zoran would have told us."

"CAN YOU PLEASE ALL STOP TALKING ABOUT MY BOYFRIEND LIKE HE'S DEAD?" Flora yelled.

"Loads of people fall under trains," Twig said.

Jas said Twig's new hobby was horrible and that Maisie Carter wasn't even pretty. Twig said she was. Jas said she wasn't. Twig said anyway, it was none of her business. Jas said he was making it her business by being so annoying.

Flora said that if they didn't shut up she'd push them both under the nearest train.

WEDNESDAY, JANUARY 1: NEW YEAR'S DAY

It's half past midnight, and it's a brand-new year.

Flora did go out with Tamsin in the end. They went into town to see the fireworks. Dodi's staying over. She said Colin had invited her to his parents' annual New Year's Eve party, but she didn't go because she knew Jake was going to be there. Grandma ordered Chinese takeout and baked a three-layer red velvet cake with cream cheese vanilla and ginger icing, and we ate the whole thing in front of the TV watching the countdown, while Jas tried to teach the kittens to ride my old skateboard. The list of things Jas is trying to teach the kittens is growing longer by the day. So far, they have failed to learn to come when they are called, to only do their business in the litter box, not to climb up curtains, and to sit on command.

"They're a lot less trainable than the rats," Jas complained. "I could get them to do almost anything."

Personally, I thought skateboarding was overly ambitious, but Twig found a sort of solution by putting Hermione on the board when she was asleep and launching her across the room before she could wake up. It didn't last very long, because she was awake within about half a second and flew from skateboard to beneath the sofa so fast she was almost just a blur, but it *was* funny. Jas said that it wasn't proper training at all, but even she laughed.

FRIDAY, JANUARY 3

Mum and Dad came home last night. Dad took Grandma to the station early this morning, but her leaving has been completely overshadowed by what has happened to Flora.

Mum and Flora both went back to bed after Grandma left, so only Twig, Jas, and I were up when the post arrived with a letter for Flora.

It came in a bright green envelope which was posted in Glasgow, and we all had a good look at it because it's quite rare for any of us to get actual mail. Then when Flora finally got up, we crowded onto the landing to watch as she picked it up from the table in the hall.

"Perhaps it's from Zach," whispered Jas.

"It's from *Scotland*," said Twig.

"Shh!" I said. Down beneath us, Flora had opened the envelope and was standing stock-still, reading. When she finished, she leaned against the wall, staring into nothing. Then she read it again.

"Do you think it *is* from Zach?" Jas insisted.

"Do you really think Zach would send a letter in a bright green envelope?" I asked.

"Perhaps it's all he could find," she said. "Perhaps it's his favorite color."

"Mum! *Mum!* MUM!" Flora yelled.

"She's still sleeping," I called down as softly as I could.

Flora tore past me into Mum's room.

"Read this!" Flora shouted, and shoved the letter under Mum's nose.

Mum moaned, "Flora, I am *asleep.*"

"Then listen!"

Flora brandished the letter, which was also bright green, waving it about until she had our full attention, and then she began to read.

"'*Dear Miss Gadsby,*

We were most impressed by your recent audition. It was a very ambitious role, and we felt that you would have tackled it well. What a shame the production coincides with your A-Level timetable, though of course it goes without saying that your exams must come first . . .'"

"I did tell you," Mum murmured, but Flora ignored her.

"'*You may know that three years ago I set up a new training facility for young actors such as yourself. Foundation courses run September to June, and I am writing now to offer you a place for next year. These places are very limited, so please let me know as soon as possible if you are interested. You will find all the relevant information concerning dates, accommodations, and fees in the accompanying information leaflet. Yours sincerely, Thomasina Foulkes-Watson.'"*

Flora was shouting louder than Grandma by the end of the letter.

"Who," Mum croaked, "is Thomasina Foulkes-Watson?"

"Thomasina Foulkes-Watson," Flora announced, "is probably the most influential talent scout, casting consultant, and producer of new plays in Britain. Her school is amazing. You have to be invited to go, and all the best actors teach there. It's like being given a place at . . . Oxford or Cambridge or Harvard or something."

"But you're going to King's." Mum was completely awake now. "They offered you a place and you're starting in October and you're going to read English and drama."

Flora stared back down at her letter before replying. She folded it very carefully and put it back in its envelope, and then she said, very softly, "No, I'm not."

She and Mum looked at each other for ages.

"No," Mum said at last. She put both her hands on her tummy, like she was asking the baby what it thought of all this, then she held one out to Flora. "No," she repeated. "I can see you're not."

I crept down to the kitchen with Twig and Jas. Twig hasn't baked anything for a while, but I found a packet of chocolate biscuits in the cupboard. We squeezed up on the sofa to eat them.

"It's all very exciting," I said.

"She's going to live in Scotland?" asked Jas.

"I can't imagine this house without Flora," said Twig, and we were all silent for a while, trying to picture it and failing.

I just went out because as I was writing I thought I heard crying from Flora's room, and I was right. She was lying in bed, fully dressed, with the duvet over her head and her face pressed into the pillow. I thought about stroking her hair, but you can never be too sure how Flora is going to react to things like that, so I just sat down next to her instead.

"Why aren't you happy?" I asked.

"I am!" she sniffed.

"You sound it," I said. She poked her head out from under the covers. Her face was all puffy, with little salt tracks from her tears and mascara halfway down her cheeks.

"You look it too," I said. Flora sniffed even louder.

"Of course I'm happy," she said, and then her lip started to wobble again and these big fat tears began to splash down her face. I had to lean really close to work out what she was saying.

"It's Zach," she wailed finally between sobs. "If I go away to Scotland, it means we're definitely over."

"Not necessarily," I said. I didn't think it was the right time to talk to her about the fickleness of men, especially given Zach's current uncommunicative behavior. "There are loads of very successful long-distance relationships," I told her.

"Name one," Flora wailed. I said well, look at all those men who went off to the First World War and spent four years in trenches with their wives waiting faithfully for them at home. Flora said that didn't exactly make her feel better since most of them *died*, and what was she going to do if he did fall under a train and did I think that was possible?

"It's possible," I said. "But like I said the other day, I think it's very unlikely."

"Don't go," she sniffed. She wriggled to the edge of her bed and I lay down next to her.

"Boys are rubbish," I whispered.

"I know," she whispered back. "But I do love him so much. Is it true you threw a milk shake over Jake?"

"How do you know about that?"

"Tamsin's mum told us. She heard it from a friend of Jake's mum. I should have said something sooner, but you know . . ." She gave me a watery smile. "Way to go, little sister," she said. And then she started crying again.

I stayed there for ages, long after Flora stopped crying and went to sleep. I thought Dodi would probably have told everyone, but I can't believe it's got as far as Tamsin's mum. There are just two days left till school starts again. Basically, someone has to do something massively dramatic, or the whole world is going to be talking about me.

Flora flipped over in her sleep and nearly hit me in the face. I slipped out from under her duvet and pulled it up around her shoulders. I wish there was something I could do for her, but I don't think an accidental meeting in the park would work a second time.

SATURDAY, JANUARY 4

I have found out why Zach means so much to Jas. She told me everything when we went back to the stables this afternoon and were brushing our horses down afterward. Their stalls are side by side, with wooden bars you can talk through, and Jas said could she ask me a question. Then she asked did I think Zach and Flora had split up, and if so, did that mean we would never see Zach again?

I said I didn't know.

"Do you think they will?"

I said maybe, when she goes to Scotland. I'd like to think mere distance wouldn't come between them, but look at me and Jake. I mean I know Australia is a lot farther than Scotland, but he was gone less than a month and he fell in love with Talullah *on the second day*. And then I heard Jas sniff and I asked, "Are you crying?" and she said no, she was perfectly fine, just a bit allergic to horses.

"That's ridiculous," I said, and then she started to cry properly.

"I tried to call him!" she sniffed. "I got his number from Flora's phone, but he didn't answer, and I left a message but he hasn't called back, and I *need* him!"

I really thought I knew what was wrong with her then. I wanted to say to her, "It's perfectly natural to have a crush on your older sister's boyfriend, trust me it happens all the time," except I wasn't sure if she knew about me liking Flora's old boyfriend Joss last year, and if she didn't I would rather it stayed that way.

"He's the only one who ever LISTENS to me," Jas cried through her tears. And that is when she told me everything, and it is nothing I would have guessed in a million years.

Jas is a poet.

And Zach is the only person who has ever read her poems.

"He really liked them," she said. "He said I had 'definite talent.' He was going to . . ."

"Going to what?" I asked.

"There's this competition," Jas said. "I read about it in the newspaper. He was helping me with it, and now I've got to the actual final, and I have to *perform* it, stand up and recite it and everything, and I DON'T KNOW WHAT TO DO!"

I stared at her in astonishment.

"That's wonderful, Jas," I told her.

"But what am I going to do?" she cried

"About what?"

"I asked you for help before but you weren't interested," Jas said. "Nobody is *ever* interested. It's all oh *my boyfriend my acting career my hair gel my documentary my baby*. It's never, EVER about me. Zach is the only one who cared and even he must have been pretending because now he's GONE!"

"Do you mind about the baby?" I asked.

"Of course not!" she said. "Do you?"

"Of course not," I said.

"I'm just sick of being the youngest," said Jas. "It used to be fun, but then you get left behind. At least once the baby's born people might stop treating me like a little kid and leave me alone."

Jas is clearly as confused about the baby as I am.

"When we get home," I said, "let's tell the parents about the competition. Dad's a writer. Maybe he can help."

"If you tell Mum and Dad I write poetry," Jas said, "I swear I will never, ever speak to you again."

My pony was growing restless. I'd stopped brushing her to talk to Jas, and I think she was wondering what I was still doing in her box. She nudged me with her head like she was pushing me toward the door.

"I don't understand why you need Zach," I said. "I mean, I can understand you're sad he's not around to hear about it and everything, but you're in the final now. I bet you'll even win."

"I can't win."

"You might."

"I CAN'T!!!" Jas shouted, and then she started talking really, really slowly, like I was really, really stupid. "This is not a children's competition. It is the West London Poetic Society's Annual Open to All Competition, but it is *not* 'open to all' because it is for people aged sixteen years and over. I can't win, BECAUSE I AM NINE YEARS OLD. It is *spectacularly* unfair."

"But why do you need Zach?" I asked.

"I need Zach," Jas said, "to pretend to be me."

Flopsy gave up on nudging, and nipped me on the shoulder. It hurt. I yelled. Flopsy pushed me out of the box.

Bill was sitting on a bench right outside the door, polishing a bridle. "You want to be more careful around horses," he said.

I stuck my head out of the top half of the door.

"Were you *listening*?" I cried, and he shrugged and said, "Sounds like someone needs to have a word with this lad." He looked straight at me when he said that.

"Me?" I asked.

"Someone's got to," he said.

"He's not answering his phone," I told him.

"More than one way of talking to a person," he said.

SUNDAY, JANUARY 5

I spent ages writing to Zach.

I wrote loads about understanding how strange it must have been to see his mum again after so long, and how hurtful her leaving must have been.

I wrote about Iris and how I know what it feels like to miss someone you really love.

I wrote about how annoying Flora can be, and how when they quarreled she was probably a load more hurtful than she told me.

Then I got annoyed, because even though this is Zach and not Jake, I am still wasting my time worrying about finding the right thing to say to a boy, and I limited my letter to facts.

"I'm truly sorry about your mum," I wrote. "But the point is, we are here, and she is not. We miss you, and we are not going away."

Then I wrote about Flora and how much she missed him and hadn't stopped moping since he went away, and about Jas, and how upset *she* was because of her poetry recital. I finished by telling him if he wanted to finish with Flora, he should be brave enough to do it properly, and otherwise he should come around and see her immediately.

"PS," I added. "Flora *is* upset, but she may choose to play it cool. I recommend flowers and chocolate."

I wrote the letter very late last night and got up early this morning to cycle over to Zoran's flat before anyone was awake to ask me what I was doing. With school starting tomorrow, I assumed they would be back soon, if they weren't back already. After I'd put it through the letter box, I sat and stared at the letter box for a while, wondering if I'd done the right thing, and then I decided there was nothing I could do about it anyway, so I came home.

At lunchtime, Mum got a phone call from Zoran, saying they were back in London.

At two thirty, Flora announced that she was going to bed with a fever and that she might never get up again.

At five minutes past four, the doorbell rang, and it was Zach, clutching a bunch of tulips. Twig answered the door, which was good, because anyone else would have made a fuss. All Twig did was say, "Oh, cool, you're back," and yell upstairs for Flora.

Flora didn't play it cool.

She appeared at the top of the stairs much too quickly for someone dying of a fever. Zach held up the flowers. Until today I never truly understood what people meant when they said "she flew down the stairs." One second Flora was on the landing, the next she was in the hall with her arms around Zach's neck. Her feet didn't touch a single step.

"You don't hate me!" she cried.

"I brought chocolate too," Zach said, and then they didn't speak for a while because they were too busy kissing. Then Jas appeared, and Zach was all, "Hey, Jas," and she said, "You're back!" Zach said, "Yeah, and we've got work to do," and Jas beamed, and then Mum waddled down from her room (the waddling is quite new, something to do with the baby pressing down between her legs, which I don't really want to think about), and then Dad came out of his study with the mad hair he gets when his writing is going badly, looking grumpy because he'd been interrupted, and even Twig left his comics, and it was impossible to get a sensible word out of anyone.

Whatever problem Zach had with our family, he has clearly gotten over it.

He came to find me later, before Zoran came around for dinner, when Flora was in the kitchen helping Mum and singing her head off. I was finishing *Jane Eyre* (and why does Mr. Rochester have to be blind at the end, why?) when he turned up in my room and not quite looking at me said thank you for the letter.

"That's okay," I said, not quite looking at him either. Then, because he was just hanging around in the doorway, I said, "Do you want to sit down," and he went and sat on my window seat.

"It's funny," he said. "First that video, then the letter. It's like you're writing my life for me."

"I do want to be a writer," I told him. "And a filmmaker."

"Well, I just wanted to say it really helped. The stuff about you all missing me, and being here and everything," he said. Then he didn't speak for ages and I was wondering if it would be all right to go back to *Jane Eyre*, when he said, "Just for the record, I never wanted to break up with Flora. I was really upset, but the reason I never called her was I threw my phone in the sea."

"That was extreme," I said.

"Mum wasn't answering my calls, and it just did my head in. So I threw it like a skimming stone. I made it bounce four times. It was kind of awesome."

"I wish I'd seen it."

Zach smiled that slow amazing smile that always reminds me why Flora likes him so much, except I think it was a little bit sadder than it used to be.

"Just don't tell Zoran," he said. "He doesn't know about it yet."

"Have you heard from your mum at all?" I asked. "Like on e-mail or anything?"

Zach said he hadn't. "I'm sorry," I told him. "Truly."

For a moment, I thought he was going to confide something, but then he smiled and just said, "Me too."

"There you are, Zach!" Flora appeared at my door, still beaming. "Mum wants ice cream, I have to go to the shop. Come with me!"

"We were talking!" I protested, but Zach was already on his feet, taking Flora's hand.

"Thanks again, Blue," he said before he left.

"What for?" I heard Flora ask.

"Just stuff," Zach replied, but then he turned around when he got to the top of the stairs and gave me a little wink, like we both knew it was a lot more than just stuff.

Flora came into my room again after dinner, wafting in like some sort of fairy princess who hadn't stuffed herself with homemade pizza and brownies and ice cream all evening in between dragging her boyfriend out of the room to snog him, under the impression no one else knew what she was doing. She draped herself over the end of my bed and hugged her knees to her chest, sighing.

"Did he tell you he threw his phone in the sea?" she said. "Isn't that dramatic? That's the thing about Zach. He seems so quiet, but he's very passionate."

I swear, drama is to Flora what blood is to a vampire.

"I told him about Scotland," she burbled. "Zach says, distance doesn't matter. He says he'll come and visit me and we can explore the Highlands together. He says he's going to buy a motorbike."

She drifted off to bed, and I thought about what I said to Zach, that we should try to be like her. Honestly, life would be so simple. I went into the bathroom to brush my teeth. It's windy tonight, and even though the moon is full you can't always see it because of these big clouds rushing across the sky. I opened the window and the noise was so loud, with the trees in Chatsworth Square blowing and the wind whistling around me. The moon came out. I thought I saw the shadow of a person, not moving, still as a statue by the railings, and suddenly I thought of what Flora had said, how she thought Zach's mum had been watching her in the park. I shivered.

I wonder what we would look like, if you were on the outside of our house, looking in. I wonder how it would feel.

The moon went back in and the shadow disappeared.

When I got to school this morning all everyone was talking about was how I assaulted Jake with a chocolate milk shake because he had two-timed me with an Australian surfer. All through morning school people kept saying things like "nice one Blue," sniggering and making milk shake slurping noises.

"Man, I wish you'd recorded it," Tom smirked. "I'd pay money to watch it."

Jake, who I thought would be mortified, has turned into a sort of minor celebrity. He looked really sheepish when he saw me this morning, in fact he went quite red, but in French when Rohan told him to "*déplacez-vous* out of my seat or *je vais jeter un milk shake over vous*," he laughed and high-fived him.

"Don't they have anything better to talk about?" I asked Dodi at break. It was freezing and most people stayed inside, but I made her sit in the playground so we wouldn't be interrupted. The boys were all playing football in the sports cage, but I kept us out of sight by hiding behind the music rooms.

"Better than you lobbing cold milky drinks around in cafés? I don't think so."

Dodi is loving the reflected glory of being my best

friend right at this moment. I wouldn't be surprised if she was going around telling people the whole thing was her idea in the first place.

"It's the best story they've had since Flora's YouTube video," she said smugly. Then she got all businesslike. "Actually, we need to talk. I left about two hundred messages on your stupid home answering machine last night."

"Nobody ever listens to those," I told her.

"Well you should. This is important. Guess what? It worked!"

"What are you talking about?" I asked.

"The milk shake throwing! Jake says you were brilliant. He says he never realized you cared so much."

"I didn't do it to impress him," I objected. "It was a genuine act of anger."

"He wants to get back together with you," Dodi said. "He rang me to ask what he should do. If you'd called me back like I asked you would know all this."

"But Talullah!" I said.

"Talullah was a mistake," Dodi said. "Now he wants to be with you."

"Well I don't want to be with him!" I cried. "I can't believe you're even talking about this!"

Dodi said that Jake was really sorry, that he was almost crying on the phone, and that he really liked me.

"He's desperate for you to forgive him," she said.

"He can't be that desperate. He's even laughing about the whole thing in a different language."

Dodi said that was just Jake saving face. She said Jake was too shy to talk to me about it himself, and she thought it was very brave of him to admit his mistakes. Jake behaved like an idiot, Dodi said, but he is basically a lovely person, and me and him were her favorite couple, and I should look out for Science, because she had heard rumors he was going to ask me to be his lab partner.

I did another thing today that I have never done before. I lied to the school nurse about having a headache and spent the whole of Science hiding in the sickroom.

TUESDAY, JANUARY 7

Now that we have sorted out the first of our problems, which was Flora and Zack, we have to deal with the second, which is Jas. After that, when everyone is happy again and I am free to live my life without the threat of imminent drowning in a lake of other people's tears, perhaps we can sort out what I'm supposed to do about Jake.

Zack and Jas's latest arrangement before he disappeared was this: because Jas is technically too young to perform—

almost half the minimum required age—Zach is going to *pretend to be her* right up until the last moment, when he will stand to one side and she will slip onto the stage. She still won't be allowed to win, she says, but at least she will have made her point.

To say that Flora, who now knows everything, is happy with this arrangement is like saying Dad wasn't furious when he discovered Ron was using his favorite suede shoes as a toilet. Jas said at least he wasn't doing it on the carpet anymore, but it didn't stop the shouting.

"Your name is *Jasmine*," Flora said to Jas. "It's a girl's name. And Zach is not a girl."

"I registered as Jas," Jas said. "It could be short for Jason."

Flora ignored her.

"It's bad enough you pretending you are nine," she told Zach, "without also making out that you are a girl."

"I think you're missing the point," I said, but she ignored me too.

"*I* will pretend to be Jas," she declared. "At least I'm the right gender."

"I can't do it without Zach," Jas said, and her voice was really shaky. I admit that at the start of this whole business I thought that two performance artists were more than one family could cope with, especially when you factor in Dad's artistic temperament and Mum's hormones as well, but when Jas said she couldn't do it without Zach I remembered how different she and Flora actually are.

"You don't have to do this," I told her.

"Of course she does," Flora said. "She's started, hasn't she? She can't give up halfway through."

The performance is less than two weeks away, and since Flora can't take to the stage in this particular role, she has appointed herself director. She has given Jas five days to prepare, and then she has to perform in front of an audience.

"And be ready to receive constructive criticism," Flora said.

"You scare me," Zach said.

"Me too," whispered Jas, but unlike Zach she wasn't laughing.

FRIDAY, JANUARY 10

If Jas really was overlooked before—and personally I have my doubts about this—she certainly isn't anymore, because the other thing Flora has insisted on is telling Mum and Dad.

"You clever, clever girl!" Mum (literally) cried, while Dad mumbled that he too was very proud and did we know that as a young man he also wrote poetry? Mum said we didn't need reminding and that for once this really wasn't about him, and then she asked Jas if many of her friends had entered the competition as well.

Flora may not have been completely honest about everything.

"The point is," she said, "it's Jas's big night, and we must all be there."

Mum and Dad said they wouldn't miss it for the world. Jas looked like she might be sick. Mum made her soup and a hot-water bottle and told her she didn't have to go to school.

The person who doesn't get any attention in this family is not Jas, but me. And maybe Twig, but he enjoys it because it means he can impress Maisie with his babysitting skills without anyone asking where he is going. I, on the other hand, would welcome some advice because I am now being stalked by Jake. He has taken to leaving me notes saying things like "I'm sorry" and "Friends?" and "I just want things to be like they were before." Dodi denies all participation. If she's lying, which I'm pretty sure she is, it might be her putting the notes in my bag and coat pocket. If she really doesn't have anything to do with it, then Jake is finding a way of doing it, which is creepy.

Rehearsals for Jas's poetry recital are in full swing, which you would think the dictator, I mean director, would be happy about except she isn't, because Jas has refused to let Flora coach her and has insisted that Zach do it. "He is *my* boyfriend," Flora complained tonight after he and Jas disappeared upstairs to her room. "She is completely monopolizing him. Seriously, he is totally neglectful. I'm beginning to regret that I agreed to help."

"When you say you agreed to help," Twig said, "did anyone actually ask you?"

I was tempted to add that Flora had no idea what it means to have a neglectful boyfriend, except Zach had come downstairs again and was already making my point for me with a very extended good-night kiss.

Until now Jas has refused to tell us anything at all about her poem, but tonight Flora beat it out of her, and I only just mean that metaphorically.

"If you don't tell me what you and Zach are up to," Flora said, "I will tell everyone, Mum, Dad, and the organizers, that you are only nine years old."

Twig said, surely Mum and Dad already knew that Jas was nine years old. Flora said he was really starting to get on her nerves this evening and whose side was he on? Jas said that while blackmail was despicable and Flora horrible, she was prepared to reveal her secret, which is that Zach has been helping her rehearse by setting her poem to music.

"What, that's it?" said Flora.

"Not setting exactly," Jas went on. "Zach says that he is helping me find the poem's rhythm. It's more that he helps me pick out the rhythms in the poem by playing them on his guitar. Then when I perform, I just have to imagine the music in my head. Zach says it is all to do with the inherent musicality of the text."

We all just stared at her.

"Oh my God," Flora said. "Zach's created a monster."

"Thank you," said Jas.

Zoran says Zach is writing songs again. When he isn't helping Jas or kissing Flora or playing soccer with Twig, he does the same as Jas and scribbles away in a corner. I asked what he was working on and Zoran said apparently it is completely different from his earlier work, which was very emotional and dark, and that he is trying to write a song that is perfectly happy but that this is much more difficult than you might think.

"It's about Flora," Zoran said. We were sitting on the veranda, even though it was cold and nearly dark. Flora was hanging off the edge of the tree house with her sweatshirt riding up almost all the way to her bra. Zach was standing underneath her, looking up and grinning.

"Have you heard from his mum?" I asked, and he said, "No, still nothing."

"What's happened to his mum?" I asked.

Zoran shrugged and said she had vanished again.

"And what about Mr. Rudowski? Did you speak to him again?"

Zoran said yes he had, but he wasn't comfortable talking to me about it, because it was inappropriate.

"But I want to know," I said.

"It's private, and it's not fair to Zach."

I thought about this for a bit. "I think it's not fair to Zach if you *don't* tell us," I said at last. "How else are we supposed to understand what he's going through?"

Zoran sighed. "She's ill, Blue, and she's incredibly possessive of Zach. She hates to see him with other people, even though she's never around."

"But I still don't understand . . ."

"People like that need help, but they don't always want it. It's hard for them and it's hard for the people around them. It killed Mrs. Rudowski."

"Wanda killed Zach's grandmother?"

"I didn't say that." Zoran smiled faintly. "I just meant that worrying about her daughter didn't help Mrs. Rudowski's cancer. And now that's enough. I don't want to talk about it anymore."

Zoran looked exhausted. I gave him a nudge.

"He looks all right now," I said, nodding at Zach gazing up at nearly naked Flora. Zoran laughed.

"I just have one last question," I told him, and he groaned.

"Flora says Zach's mother was watching her when she was with Zach. And the other night, I thought I saw her outside the house. Don't you think that's weird?"

"I think that one day, with that fine imagination of yours, you're going to make a very fine writer," Zoran said.

"No, but seriously," I said.

"Seriously. A great writer."

He nudged me back, and I couldn't help laughing.

It was nice, sitting there and believing that.

THE FILM DIAIRIES OF BLUEBELL GADSBY
SCENE SEVEN (TRANSCRIPT)
DRESS REHEARSAL

The Gadsby living room. Chairs are arranged in two neat rows upon which sit FLORA, ZACH, TWIG, DODI, and ZORAN. All the lamps in the room have been assembled by the piano, where JAS stands in a pool of light, looking like the proverbial trapped bunny. The rest of the room is in darkness.

> (Applause)
>
> JAS
>
> Shall I start?

> FLORA
>
> Don't say "shall I start." Survey the room and wait for silence. Command our attention. Then, when you have it, begin.

DODI

(whispering, to Twig)

How's it going with Maisie?

TWIG

(whispering back)

What's it to you?

DODI

(trying not to snigger)

Just that I heard she was hanging out with Justin
Murphy after school last Wednesday.

TWIG

(a lot more loudly)

I heard you don't know how to mind your own
business.

ZORAN

(in a very loud stage whisper)

Please show respect to your sister and be quiet.

JAS, to everyone

I actually don't see the point of this rehearsal at
all.

FLORA

SILENCE IN THE HOUSE, PLEASE!

JAS

I can't do this.

ZACH

Of course you can.

JAS

I really can't.

Zach rises to whisper in her ear. Jas gulps, nods, takes
a deep breath, and tilts her chin as she turns back to
face the camera. She opens her mouth to begin, but is
put off by a scuffling noise from behind the door.

TWIG

(whispers)

I bet that's the parents listening.

*NOTE: parents have been banned from the rehearsal on
the grounds that grown-ups will only make Jasmine even
more nervous.*

Flora frowns and steps toward the door. The scuffling stops.

Flora orders Jasmine to continue, but Jasmine is already at the door, which she flings open. PARENTS tumble into the room as Jasmine runs out.

Zach, after a brief hesitation, goes after her. Flora starts to follow them, but he shakes his head and she remains.

Camera goes black.

SUNDAY, JANUARY 12

The room stayed silent for about fifteen seconds and then it exploded.

"What were you *thinking*?" Flora yelled at the parents. "You put her off the whole rehearsal!"

"It was your father's idea," Mum mumbled. "I didn't want to listen."

"And yet there you were. Listening," Flora pointed out.

"It's not fair to exclude us," Dad declared.

I explained about adults making Jas nervous.

"Zoran's here!" Dad protested.

"He's not a real adult," Flora said.

The whole point of filming was for Jas to watch herself afterward and correct any mistakes. "We'll have to do it again," Flora said, but when Jas finally came back down, she just said no, she knew what was wrong and she was on it.

"No more rehearsals," she said.

"But you're not ready . . ." Flora started to say, and then Zach wandered into the room with his guitar.

"Tell them," Jas ordered.

"We're good," Zach said, and that is when I knew that Zach is exactly the right boyfriend for Flora, because even though he doesn't shout and he's not particularly cool or tough like some of her previous boyfriends, all he has to do is shuffle into a room and say "we're good" and she shuts up.

Zoran took me aside. "You know she can't go through with this," he said. "Even if they don't disqualify her because of her age, they'll eat her alive."

"She'll be fine," I said.

"Unlike your parents, I do my research! She's a *child*, for God's sake! She's competing against adults. I don't approve of this secrecy. I've a good mind to tell them what's going on."

"Jas is changing," I said. "If she has decided she wants to do this, no one can stop her."

Today I found two red roses in my locker. Dodi admitted almost immediately that she had given Jake the combination to my lock.

"You have to stop encouraging him," I told her.

"But he loves you so much!" she cried.

"This is getting ridiculous," I said. "When I like him, he doesn't like me. Now that I don't like him, he does like me. Why is that?" Dodi said she didn't know, but that it was a shame, and maybe it was because opposites attract.

"So if I'm nice to him, he might go off me?" I asked.

"I still don't understand why you *want* him to go off you," Dodi said. "I think he's lovely."

"Because he's ANNOYING!" I cried. "And if you like him so much, why don't *you* go out with him?"

Dodi went a bit red and said, "It's not me he likes," and I felt mean because Dodi doesn't like to be reminded that she's never had a boyfriend.

"Well he's an idiot," I said, and she cheered up a bit.

I thanked Jake for the flowers as we waited to go into Math.

"It was very thoughtful of you," I said. It was the first time I'd spoken to him since the Milk Shake Incident, and his whole face lit up like it was on fire.

"Did you like them?" he asked.

"They were very pretty," I said, and then I went to sit right at the back of the class by the window, where none of the teachers allow him to go.

"I'm coming to your sister's performance on Sunday!" he called out as Mr. Math came in.

"Whenever you're ready, Jake," said Mr. Math.

Maybe my theory is wrong. Sometimes, if you're nice to people, it only makes them like you more.

SUNDAY, JANUARY 19

Zach and Zoran were late. They were meant to meet us at home at six thirty, but by quarter to seven Dad said we couldn't wait any longer. He phoned Zoran and told him we were leaving and to meet us at the recital. He also told him to get his act together because this was the most important night of his daughter's life and she needed all the support she could get.

"Stop being so jumpy," Flora said. "You're only making her more nervous."

Dad said he couldn't help it. He said he felt responsible for Jas, because she must have inherited her writing genes from him. Mum reminded him that this wasn't about him.

"I'm sure there's a good reason for their lateness," she added, but Dad still wouldn't calm down. "They are selfish, thoughtless, and incompetent," he said as he tried to bundle us out of the house.

Twig announced Jas had just run upstairs to be sick.

The West London Open Evening of Poetry took place in a church with salmon-pink walls and dark green woodwork and paintings of angels in gold and blue above the altar, which sounds hideous but wasn't, as I had plenty of time to observe through what for the most part was a long, dull evening. The first thing I noticed when we went in was how big it was. Also, how many people in West London appeared to like poetry, and how old everyone was compared to Jas. I don't think I ever realized how young nine was before tonight. A lot of the people in the room looked like our next door neighbors, Mr. and Mrs. Bateman, who are way past sixty and wear beige and do a lot of gardening, or else they were people Mum's and Dad's age in long colorful shawls and no makeup, who looked as though they might like to walk barefoot through fields on beautiful dewy mornings, chanting hymns of praise to the sunrise. There was a man in his twenties pacing up and down waving his arms doing some last minute rehearsing, and a girl wearing a nose ring and a yellow jumpsuit who looked a bit confused, but there was absolutely nobody as small and terrified as Jas.

"Tickets are ten pounds each," said a lady in a maroon dress with long gray hair and no bra. "Are you here to support one of the acts?"

"Where are all the other children?" asked Mum.

The ticket lady looked baffled, but we'd rehearsed this. Flora took control. "Jas Gadsby," she said to the ticket lady, and at the same time she turned toward the parents. "Dad, why don't you give me the money for the tickets and take Mum to sit down?"

"You do look tired, Mum," said Twig.

"Let me help you," I offered as Flora reached into Dad's pocket for his wallet.

"Well come along, young star!" Dad draped his arm around Jas's shoulders. "Where do the performers sit?" he asked.

"Anywhere near the front." The ticket lady still looked puzzled.

Jas took her seat in a daze and said she was going to be sick again.

"Keep it in, shrimp," said Flora, when she joined us. "This is your big night."

"I still don't understand why there aren't any other children," Mum said.

"Your boyfriend's here, by the way," Flora smirked at me.

"I don't have a boyfriend," I said.

"Tell him that. He's sitting two rows back."

I sneaked a look and it was true. Just across the aisle, two rows back, Jake and Dodi were sitting together. Dodi beamed. Jake gave a little wave, then blushed scarlet. I turned back around to the front.

"I'm going to kill her," I muttered. "I didn't think he would actually come."

Flora snorted.

Zoran slid onto the end of our bench just as the lights were dimming.

"Where have you *been*?" Flora asked. For all her stomping about, she was almost as nervous as Jas.

"Everything's fine," Zoran said.

"And where is Zach?"

"He *is* coming, isn't he?" Jas whispered.

"I'm here." Zach slid in next to Zoran, who put his arm around his shoulders.

"All right, mate?" I heard him ask.

"Yeah, fine," Zach answered. Zoran squeezed him and let him go.

"Do we have to be so squashed up?" asked Twig.

I feel a little sad writing it, because I hate to give up on anything, but I'm not sure poetry will ever be my thing. The long-haired brightly shawled ladies came and went, along with the gray-haired, beige cardigan–wearing older people. The young man in the business suit cried as he recited a poem written when his wife got married for the second time. "Not to me," he added, in case we hadn't understood why he was sad.

"This *isn't* a children's competition!" Mum remarked. Dad gulped and looked like *he* was going to be sick.

"Jas will be absolutely fine," Zoran said firmly.

The girl in the yellow jumpsuit must have realized she was in the wrong place and vanished without a trace. Twig and I both fell asleep and were woken by Flora with a sharp elbow in the ribs because the master of ceremonies had just called out Jas's name and she was rising from her seat, white as a ghost and shaking like a leaf, staring at the front of the church with Zach standing next to her holding his guitar.

"Ready?" he mouthed. Jas tried to smile.

"Jas Gadsby!" The master of ceremonies called again, and Jas and Zach walked down the aisle together, Jas in her usual uniform of black dress and leggings and silver high-tops and Zach with his guitar on his back.

"I don't understand." The master of ceremonies frowned when they reached the front.

"Neither do I," murmured Dad.

Flora sighed as Zach reached out to take Jas's hand.

Jas suddenly seemed to grow about six inches and took the microphone.

"Just because I am nine years old," she announced, "does not mean I can't write poetry."

A lot of people started to laugh. Dad put his head in his hands. Zach smiled, stepped onto the stage, and began to play. Jas stood very still at the front of the stage looking tiny, waited for the audience to be silent, and began.

> *There is a gravestone where I like to sit . . .*
> *A stony relic of one long dead.*
> *Something about it seems to fit*
> *The creature that lives inside my head.*

"She's good!" Dad breathed.

"It rhymes," Twig whispered.

"Shut up, both of you," Flora hissed.

Jas went on, Zach still strumming softly along with her.

> *Around the graveyard the city roars*
> *The steady beat of human living.*
> *Deep inside a creature claws,*
> *A creature who is not forgiving.*

This creature belongs to the night.
This creature shies away from light.
This creature must keep out of sight,
Who lives inside my head.

The grave is strewn with moss and flowers.
Here birds can sometimes come to nest.
I sit here often and for hours.
Here the beast inside me likes to rest.

I know I'm biased and also that I slept through a lot of others, but Jas's number was the best by far. She and Zach repeated the *This creature belongs to the night* verse several times together, like a chorus, so it sounded more like a song than a poem, and maybe that, as well as it being Zach and Jas, is why I liked it. But I wasn't the only one. There was a moment of stunned silence at the end, because I'm not sure the audience was expecting something quite so dark from one so young, but then they were all on their feet, cheering. A journalist from the local paper was trying to take photographs and write in his notebook at the same time. Jas beamed and hugged Zach, who grinned and hugged her back. Dad yelled, "That's my daughter! That's my daughter!" punching the air with his fist; Twig and Flora and I jumped up and down on our seats to get a better look;

Zoran held Mum as she cried her eyes out. Behind us I could hear Dodi and Jake cheering too.

"She was amazing!" Dodi yelled when I turned around.

"Amazing!" Jake echoed. I forgot about him being creepy and waved.

A lot of the time my family drive me mad, but tonight wasn't like that. Tonight was absolutely brilliant.

She didn't win, of course, just as Zoran said she wouldn't. First prize went to one of the shawled ladies for a sonnet about cats, and the second prize went to one of the old men for a ballad about the love of his life being like a vampire, which made the young man in the suit cry even more. Afterward, just before the local journalist asked to take a photograph of all of us, the competition organizers gave Mum and Dad and Jas a long lecture about all the rules she had broken, and how she had abused their trust by entering false details, and how this disqualified her from winning. "But your work shows promise," the lady organizer said, with what I think was the most patronizing smile I have ever seen. "I am sure you will mature into a very interesting young poet."

Flora blew a raspberry behind her back. We all laughed. Gloria and Bill turned up, Bill still looking like a bum, Gloria stunning in head to toe tight-fitting black. She told Jas her poetry was even better than her riding and Jas beamed even more. Dad and Zoran both gaped at Gloria. Twig sniggered. The local reporter took our photograph, and we all spilled out of the church into the night. Zach lifted Jas onto his shoulders and she screeched for him to put her down, but she was still laughing. Flora stood on tiptoe to kiss him on the lips. Mum leaned on Dad's arm, and they were both laughing.

It was brilliant.

And then everything changed.

The stone caught Mum just above her right temple. She stumbled, slipped, and crashed to the ground. Someone screamed, I still don't know who. Jas tumbled down from Zach's shoulders, but he caught her in his arms before she hit the pavement. A man pushed through the crowd of people coming out of the church saying he was a doctor, and knelt beside Mum, who was lying with her head in Dad's lap.

"I'm all right," Mum murmured. Her head was bleeding.

"My wife is pregnant!" Dad cried.

The doctor leaned over to take Mum's pulse. For a minute, because he smiled at her, I thought everything was going to be all right. Then he looked at Dad and told him to call an ambulance.

No one saw who did it, but I know. And I'm not the only one.

It's so obvious.

Dad went to the hospital in an ambulance with Mum last night, while Zoran drove us home in our car. Zach sat with him in the front, with Flora and the others in the row behind them. I sat in the back.

Jas was crying and asking questions. "Why would anyone do that? Why Mummy? Why here, why tonight, why now?"

"I don't know," Flora answered.

I thought about the baby, the feel of its head under my hand on Mum's tummy, the jab when it kicks, Mum saying "imagine how it feels for me?" Mum on Christmas Day, snoring on the sofa, and playing charades on Boxing Day. I wanted to say something but I couldn't speak. Literally. It was like the connection between my brain and my mouth was broken.

If anything happens to them . . . I clenched my fists till my nails dug into my palms. If I wasn't writing this, I'd still be clenching them now.

"Who would do that?" Jas sobbed, and Flora said again

that she didn't know. But I know, and Zoran knows, and Zach knows who threw the stone at Mum.

Neither of them talked the whole way home, but at one point Zoran reached out to squeeze Zach's shoulder again, like he did before. I was too far away to hear what he said but it sounded like a question. Zach shrugged and looked out of the window. He looked like he wanted to cry, and I thought "good."

I wish we'd never met him and his stupid mother. I wish Zoran had never agreed to look after him.

Zoran dropped Zach off first before taking us home, and then he said he'd stay with us until Dad got back. Flora told him he didn't have to, but he said he wanted to.

We didn't go to bed. Instead we brought our duvets down to the living room, where we huddled together on the sofa and waited. It was after two when Dad got home. Everybody was asleep except me and Zoran, sitting together in the dark, still not talking. Dad sat down with us on the sofa. The others woke up and we all crawled over to him.

"How's Mum?" Twig asked.

"All right, but they're keeping her under observation."

"What about the baby?" asked Flora.

"We'll know more tomorrow."

I pressed in closer to him. I was vaguely aware of a hand on my shoulder, Zoran murmuring, "I'll call in the morning." I thought he might tell Dad then, but he didn't say a word, and neither did I.

We all went upstairs, but once the others were in bed I crept back down again. I found Dad in his study, sitting at his desk with his head in his hands, surrounded by papers.

"I thought I'd try to work," he said. "I knew I wouldn't be able to sleep."

I moved a stack of books from the armchair in the corner and curled up in it.

"How is your book going?" I asked.

"Badly," Dad said. Then he said that it hardly mattered anymore.

"I swear to God, if anything happens to them . . ." His voice was shaking. He pressed his hands down on his desk, like doing that was the only thing stopping him from throwing everything on the floor or ripping up all those precious sheets of paper.

"I know," I said.

"If anything happens to your mother or that baby," he said in a steadier voice, "I will find the person who did this thing and I will make him pay. I will rip him to pieces. I will tear off his head."

"Dad," I said.

"I will pull out his heart and stamp on his guts and . . ."

"Dad, you're scaring me!"

He was prowling around his study now, punching his right fist into the palm of his left hand. He stopped right in front of me and looked at me like he hadn't seen me properly until then.

"I'll kill him," he said.

I can't talk to him when he's like this. I spoke to Flora instead. I found her sitting on her bed with her arms wrapped round her knees, staring at her phone. I sat next to her, but she didn't look up.

"I think it was Zach's mother," I whispered.

She carried on staring at her phone.

"It has to be," I insisted. "Who else would do something like that? She's mad, Flora. Zoran says she killed her own mother."

"Zach's gran died of cancer."

"You saw her in the park," I went on. "Remember? I've seen her too. I'm sure I have. She's been watching us, Flora. She's jealous and she hates us."

"I'm not even sure it was her I saw," Flora said tonelessly. "And even if I did, it doesn't mean anything. It's not proof."

"Flora, Mum's in hospital!"

She looked up at last, and I saw that she had been crying. "Does it matter?" she asked. "You heard what Dad said,

Mum's all right. I don't want to fight with Zach again."

"So you do think it was her!"

She didn't answer for ages.

"We have to do something," I said. "What if she does it again?"

"I don't want to talk about it."

She lay down and pulled the duvet over her head. I waited for her to say something else, but she didn't and I left her too.

I don't know what to do.

MONDAY, JANUARY 20 (CONT.)

I'm writing this from Zoran's front doorstep. None of us went to school today.

The police came this morning. There were two of them, a man who didn't look like we interested him very much at all and a woman who kept calling us "dear." They said, they were sorry to intrude on us when we must be so preoccupied but they just had a few questions and perhaps the younger children would rather not be present? The way they said it made it obvious they were the ones who had much rather Jas and Twig weren't there.

"If there is to be a police investigation," Twig said, "there is absolutely no way I will not be present."

"Me neither," Jas whispered. They had been standing by the door but now Jas took Twig's hand and led him to the sofa, where they sat together, very close, and didn't let go. The policewoman smiled, like she thought they were impossibly cute. The policeman didn't.

Dad stood by the door with his coat on, looking anxious.

Flora sat in the red armchair in her tartan pajama bottoms and the old cardigan she always wears when she's worried or upset, concentrating really hard on trying to answer the police's questions. She didn't look at me.

I thought, I have to tell them. Mum is lying in hospital, and I have to tell them what I know. But Flora was talking, saying we had no idea who could have done it and I thought, she's right, thinking something isn't proof. Last night I *thought* I knew, but that's not the same thing. And the longer Flora talked, the harder it got to say anything.

"Our mother has no enemies," said Flora. "None of us are aware of any quarrels or arguments she may have had, and nobody saw what happened."

At the end, the policewoman said they would do their best to find the culprit, but that it sounded like a random attack and that, unless he struck again, the attacker would be difficult to catch. She said that someone from Victim Support would be in touch to offer counseling. Dad said that would be great but the person who needed support right now was his wife and their unborn child, and then he pretty much ran out of the house to go to the hospital.

Jas started to cry again.

I love Dad, but I wish he were better in a crisis.

After Dad and the police had gone, I waited for Flora to say something to me, but she still didn't. And then I thought I don't care what she thinks, and I came here. Zoran is out. It's twelve thirty, and I've been sitting on this doorstep for nearly an hour. Luckily it's mild again, and sunny. There's this big tree outside Zoran's building, and the squirrels in it are going crazy, chasing one another around and around the trunk. There's a robin too, hopping about making chirping noises, and a fat old tabby cat sleeping on the wall in the sun. It seems quite incredible to me that all this is going on when Mum is lying in hospital.

Zoran just turned in from the street. Time to stop writing.

I'm clenching my fists again.

LATER

I'm in bed now. Dad called from the hospital this evening. Mum and the baby are both fine, but the doctors still want to keep her in for a few days just in case. He explained that she has been suffering from very high blood pressure and the doctors had worried that it might be something called preeclampsia. It isn't, which is a good thing because we looked it up on Google and the only cure is to deliver the baby, and if that happened it could die because it is still so small.

"I don't want the baby to die." Jas began to cry, and Twig looked like he might too.

"No one is going to die," I said.

"What if it happens again!" Jas wailed. "What if there's a murderer stalking her! What if someone is trying to kill her!"

The Jas who tears around obstacles courses on horseback and recites poetry to a packed audience has completely vanished.

"Nobody is stalking us," I said, but what if that's not true?

Zoran went to see Mr. Rudowski this morning. That's where he was when I was waiting for him on his doorstep, and that's why he didn't call us this morning like he said he would.

"Where's Zach?" I asked. Zoran said he was back at school. He said it was important to keep things as normal as possible.

"What news of Cassie and the baby?" he asked. I didn't answer.

"The police came," I said instead. "Speaking of normal."

Zoran was looking for his keys, and he didn't look at me.

"What did they say?" he asked.

"They wanted to know if Mum had enemies. Flora said no. I wanted to say yes, but I couldn't, because I wasn't sure."

"You weren't sure of what?"

"If Mum has enemies." And then I didn't know how to say what I wanted to say and we'd reached the top of the stairs and were going into Zoran's flat, and I wondered what Grandma or Dodi would do if it was them and I just blurted out, "Was it Zach's mother who did it?"

Sometimes when you don't know how to do something it's easier to pretend you're someone else.

Zoran sighed and said yes, he thought it was.

I didn't know what to say next, and I suppose Zoran didn't either, because he just stood there leaning against a wall with his arms crossed, looking at the floor and frowning.

"She came back just before the show," he said at last. "We left the house and she was waiting for us outside. She was upset. She'd finally been to the hospital to see her father and they had a fight."

"What was the fight about?"

Zoran said Wanda wouldn't say, but Mr. Rudowski told him this morning, and that the fight was about money. "To put it bluntly, Mr. Rudowski said Wanda was in trouble and she came back to get what she could before he died."

"That's horrible," I said, and Zoran agreed but said that

there was nothing like the possibility of imminent death of close relatives to bring out the worse in people.

"But if she just came back for the money, why did she want to see Zach?"

Zoran's face softened for a moment. "He's her son, Blue."

"But she's horrible to him."

"I didn't say she was logical. I just said he's her son. She's confused but she still loves him. Just as he loves her. He was so sweet with her, Blue. Put his arm around her, tried to calm her down. She was hysterical, kept saying her father had sent her away again—nothing at all about the money, obviously. Zach said he couldn't let Jas down, and asked her to come with us. He told her he'd love that. He even asked me if she could stay with us."

"But she didn't."

"Of course not. She started crying that Zach didn't love her anymore, that she'd lost everything and that it was all his and her father's fault. And then she must have followed us and waited for us to come out. You know what happened next."

Zoran said that he had wanted to tell Dad last night but Zach had begged him not to, and given what Zach had just been through and what he'd done for Jas, he agreed to wait. And then this morning he decided to go and see Mr. Rudowski.

"What did he say?" I asked.

"He begged me not to go to the police."

"But she hurt Mum! Doesn't he care?"

"She's his daughter," Zoran said gently. "And what are the police going to do?"

"Catch her!"

"She needs medical help, Blue."

"But what about Mum? What if Wanda comes back and attacks her again?"

Zoran said that he would find her. He said he would never let anything bad happen to any of us, and that was why his biggest priority now was to make sure Wanda got the help she needed from doctors and from her own family.

"We have to tell Dad," I said.

Zoran hesitated. "If that's what you want."

"Of course it's what I want! Why wouldn't we tell Dad?"

"He has a lot on his plate right now. And David can get a bit—irrational himself. I wonder if we might wait. For Zach's sake."

I thought about Dad last night, how angry he was.

"If you want to do the right thing by one person," I said, "does it always mean you are doing the wrong thing by somebody else?"

Zoran said sometimes that was the case, but not always.

"Flora knows," I told him. "But she won't admit it. She says

I'm imagining things, but really she's afraid of upsetting Zach."

"Let me find Wanda," Zoran said.

Jas is sleeping with Twig tonight. I just stopped in Flora's room on my way back from the bathroom. She hasn't asked me where I went this afternoon, and I haven't told her.

TUESDAY, JANUARY 21

We went to the hospital today. Mum is on a ward with four other women. Her window looks out over the railway tracks and her bed is separated from the others by curtains. She says it's super-cozy and all the women chat to one another and swap stories, but she looked exhausted.

Maybe Flora is feeling guilty for her silence, because she flitted about Mum's cubicle arranging flowers and plumping pillows and feeding her soup she brought from home in a thermos like she was the sort of nurse you see in black-and-white films who look like nuns.

I read out loud to her from *Jane Eyre*.

Twig told us about the trains he could see out of the window.

Jas sat on the floor because there weren't enough chairs, hugging her knees and looking sorrowful. I got to the bit where Jane traipses across the moors, lost and abandoned without a hope in the world, and she started to sniff. Twig stared at her, amazed.

"Are you crying because of the book?" he asked. "Because I think it's the stupidest thing I ever heard."

"You're just uncultured," I told him.

"Let's not quarrel," Flora murmured, and Jas howled even louder.

I asked her, "Are you really crying because of *Jane Eyre*?" and she gave a giant hiccup and wailed that NO, OF COURSE SHE WASN'T, and then she threw herself on Mum's bed shouting MUMMY MUMMY MUMMY and that it was all her fault. Mum said no no no of course it wasn't and Jas said yes yes yes it was until a nurse came along and kicked us out, telling us we'd be the death of our mum if we carried on like that, which really didn't help at all.

Jake came around this afternoon. He turned up on the doorstep with a bag full of chocolate bars and before I could even open my mouth to talk he said, "I just wanted to say I'm sorry about your mum," and I let him in. I wasn't sure what I should do with him so we sat on the stairs eating the chocolate while I told him what I could, which wasn't very much.

"It was such an awesome evening," Jake said. "Until, you

know, the attack and everything. Jas and the poetry and Flora's boyfriend, it was brilliant."

I couldn't help smiling. Jake is basically inarticulate, but I always know what he means, and he's right. Jas and the poetry and Zach *were* brilliant. Then I wished I *hadn't* smiled, because he gazed at me, all hopeful, like he thought my smile meant something completely different.

"I really like you, Blue," he said.

I couldn't think of a single thing to say. All I could think about was Mum and how she looked this afternoon and Jas screaming MUMMY MUMMY MUMMY as the nurse pushed us out of the room.

"I'm really sorry about Talullah," Jake went on. "I don't know what I was thinking. I think I went a bit crazy, remembering the beach and surfing and stuff. Like, even though we were back in England, it wasn't real life, you know?"

He looked so sorry for himself I almost started to feel sorry for him too. I love Jake in a way, I really do, but he does pick his moments to try and get philosophical.

"Can't we try again?" he asked. "You're one of my best friends, Blue. I hate that we don't talk anymore."

"You're one of my best friends too, Jake," I said, and he beamed.

"That thing you did with the milk shake was wicked," he said. "I mean, you kind of ruined my hoodie and everything, but the way you just *did* it was mad. It was like you couldn't care less what I thought."

Boys are so strange.

"So are we back together and everything?" Jake asked.

I told him, all I said was he was one of my best friends too, and he said yeah, I know, but that meant something, right?

I figure there are enough miserable people in the world. Why add to them unnecessarily? And maybe it would be nice to go out with Jake again. Maybe this time, if I didn't expect too much from it, it could work.

"I'll think about it," I said.

Jake said that was awesome.

"You'd better go now," I said. Jake said okay, and asked if I was coming back to school tomorrow. He leaned toward me but I moved away. I'm really not in the mood for more kissing practice.

"You can leave the chocolate," I said as he went to pick up the bag.

Flora says I am making a big mistake. She swooped down on the chocolate from the first floor landing the minute Jake was gone. She was listening to every word we said. She says when it comes to boys, you have to let them know exactly where they stand at all times and that it's only inviting trouble if you don't. She says that in the long run, it's kinder to be cruel.

She still hasn't said a word about Zach's mum.

WEDNESDAY, JANUARY 22

Jas announced this morning that she had had nightmares all night.

"It's true," Twig said. "She came and slept with me again."

I glared at Flora. She looked away.

I called Zoran last night, but they still haven't heard from Wanda.

On the way home from school today, Dodi repeated that she was tired of leaving messages on the house phone that no one ever answers.

"Either you buy a new phone," she said, "or we get the old one back from Madame Gilbert."

"Madame Gilbert hates me," I said, and then I switched off because Dodi started saying how the reason she called me last night was to talk about Jake, and I'm not comfortable discussing Jake right now. I think Flora may have been right about needing to be more clear. This morning there was another rose pinned to my locker, and during Math he gave me a drawing of a little dog wagging its tail and looking hopeful. I'd forgotten how good he is at drawing, but seriously, a little dog?

"You're not listening," Dodi said. She gave me this really sharp look, a bit like Grandma, and said, "Tell me everything."

"I'm not sure I'm allowed to," I said.

"Forget *that!*" she snorted.

"I *can* sort of understand Flora not wanting to stir things up with Zach," she admitted when I'd finished. We were at home now, carrying tea up to my bedroom and talking in whispers. "He seems to be pretty protective of his mum. And I guess if *your* mum's okay . . ."

"It's not right," I said. "It's like she's more loyal to Zach than to Mum. And also, what if Zach's mother does it again? Zoran says he's going to find her, but he hasn't. We *have* to tell the police."

Dodi whispered that she thought I was probably right. Then, because she can never be serious for very long, she nudged me, nearly making me spill my tea.

"I'll say one thing for Jake," she grinned. "However useless he was as a boyfriend, at least his mum isn't a known criminal. She might be a bit boring, but she's definitely not the rock-slinging type."

"It's not funny," I told her, but Dodi nudged me again, and I started to smile. "It's not a great recommendation for a boyfriend though, is it?" I said, and she agreed that the fact that Jake's mum didn't hurl stones at people probably wasn't enough of a reason to go out with him. And then we were going into my room, and Dodi jumped and this time the tea did go all over the carpet as she yelled, "WHAT ARE YOU *DOING*," at Jas who was standing on my bed like a little ball of fury, holding my diary and waving it above her head screaming, "You knew! You knew and you didn't say!"

"Give that back!" I cried, but she backed up against the wall, holding it behind her.

"I heard you!" she shouted. "You were talking about it with *Dodi*!"

"Calm down, shrimp," Dodi said. "I'm her BFF."

"I'm going to tell Daddy!" Jas screamed. She made a run for the door, but Dodi caught her. Jas tried to bite her, but Dodi is surprisingly strong.

"Dad's at the hospital." I tried to keep very calm, even though I was shaking.

"Then I'll phone him!" Jas shouted. "I'll run away! I'll tell the police!"

"Tell the police what?" Flora wandered into my room. "Why is Dodi holding Jas? What is Jas screaming about? What on earth is going on?"

"She'll come back," Jas insisted. "It's all here in Blue's book. She's mad and she hates Mum, and Zoran can't do anything to stop her!"

"What are you talking about?" Flora repeated.

"She killed her own mother!" Jas wailed. "And now she wants to kill ours."

Flora looked at me. I shrugged, and told Jas to give her my diary.

It was weird, watching Flora read. It was like she stopped breathing, like a balloon with a tiny puncture, getting smaller and smaller until she was almost completely flat.

"Why didn't you tell me you'd spoken to Zoran?" she said when she'd finished.

"You didn't want to hear," I said.

Jas said, "I'm really scared, Flora."

And even though Flora's loyalties may be divided, she's still our big sister. She started to breathe again and held her hand out to Jas.

"Come on," she said. "I think it's time to go and have a chat with Zach."

SAME DAY, MUCH LATER

I'm so tired I can barely hold my pen.

Dodi left us on the way to Zoran's flat. She may not be the most tactful person in the world, but I think even she realized that she might get in the way. Flora marched down the street in silence, still holding Jas's hand. I don't know what she was thinking as she walked, but she looked more and more angry with every step.

"It's me," Flora snapped at the intercom when Zoran answered, and then she stomped up the stairs. Zoran was waiting on the landing. He didn't even say hello. He took one look at Flora and stepped aside to let us in. Flora stormed straight into the living room.

"Stay with Blue," she ordered Jas, who transferred her hand from Flora's to mine.

The way Flora barreled into that room, I thought she was going yell and scream and try doing some of the things Dad said he wanted to do, the ripping and stamping and punching stuff. She looked like some warrior queen about to dismember invading hoards, but then Zach turned around from the window where he was standing and she stopped dead in her tracks.

Zach looks dreadful. Not just like a bit sad or worried or depressed, but truly horrible. The purple smudges under his eyes are almost black, his eyes are darker than ever, and his skin is so pale he looks like he might be dead. He was actually a bit scary, and I know Jas thought so too because she moved closer, so she was standing right up against me, but that is not the effect he had on Flora.

The effect he had on Flora was that she gasped, then

held her arms out and rushed toward him, crying, "Baby, what's happened to you!"

"I'm sorry," Zach said. "Zoran told me you knew. I'm so, so sorry about what she did. I should have said something."

"No, *I* should have said something!" Flora said. "I guessed, but I didn't want to upset you. I shouldn't have left you all alone."

Then she threw her arms around him and showered his face in kisses.

"It's not her fault," Zach said when Flora finally let him breathe again, and we were all sitting around Zoran's tiny coffee table. "She gets so jealous. I should have seen it coming."

"Of course it's not your fault!" Flora cried. She started kissing him again.

I glanced at Zoran who was frowning, looking worried. Jas moved even closer to me and whispered, "Ask him where she is now," but I had another question first.

"If she gets so jealous of you, why did she go away?" I asked. "Before, I mean, not just after Christmas."

"Leave him alone, Blue," Flora said.

"It's a valid question," Zoran murmured.

"It was Grandpa," Zach said. "Their fight, after Grandma died. He didn't give her a choice.

"She was always lovely when she came back," Zach insisted. "She does crazy things sometimes, but she's not a bad person. And she knew Gran was there to look after me. She wouldn't have left me if I hadn't had Gran."

I thought about Grandma, then. Once when we were staying with her, the vet came to see one of her ponies, who was lame. The vet said the pony should be put down. "There isn't really a choice," the vet said, but instead Grandma nursed the pony back to health. No one can ever ride him again, but Grandma says at least he's happy, living quietly in her paddock.

"There's always a choice," Grandma said.

I didn't say anything now, because it didn't seem right, but I thought it.

Jas tugged at my arm. I caught Flora's eye. She nodded, like she was saying "you do it," and laced her fingers through Zach's.

So much for the protective big sister.

"The reason we came," I said, "is that Jas is worried . . ."

"Not *just* me," Jas said.

". . . is that we're *all* worried in case Wanda, I mean your mum, attacks *our* mum again."

"You're going to find her, aren't you, Zach?" said Flora.

"He hasn't found her so far," I pointed out.

"But he will," she replied.

Zoran crouched down in front of Jas. "I promise nothing

bad is going to happen again," he said. "But just so you feel really safe, shall we go and tell your dad everything?"

"And call the police?" said Jas.

"If that's what he wants to do." He glanced over at Zach. "I'm sorry, but this has gone far enough," he said. "Cassie and the baby might be out of danger, but I'm not having Jas going around frightened."

The house felt different when we got home. Dad had put the heat right up, and there was a big bunch of flowers on the table in the hall. "Mummy's flowers from the hospital!" Jas cried. "She's back!"

She ran upstairs. Flora and I followed. Mum was lying in bed, looking tired but happy in her old pink dressing gown, with a cup of tea and a plate of biscuits on a tray, Twig, Ron, and Hermione lying beside her, and Dad beaming over them, wearing an apron and looking surprisingly like an old mother hen.

"You're better!" Jas flung herself onto the bed. Mum laughed and reached out to hug her.

I always knew Dad would react badly. After we'd all hugged Mum, Flora said Zach and Zoran were downstairs. Mum said they should come up. "After all," Mum said, "they are part of this family too." Zach and Zoran came in, looking nervous. Zoran explained.

"I'm sorry," Zoran said. "I should have said something

earlier. It's just . . . It's been difficult." Mum put her hand on his arm. "Dear Zoran, you're not telling me anything I didn't already suspect."

My mum's amazing.

Zoran pressed his forehead against her hand and murmured, "Thank you."

"The thing to do now is find her." Mum reached out to Zach. "You poor thing, you look so tired."

And it could have ended there, except that's when Dad shouted, "No!"

Everyone turned to look at him. "No, no, no!" he repeated. "You all knew and you never said anything? Blue knew, and Flora knew, and Zoran knew, and you knew, and nobody thought to tell me? I have spent days *out of my mind* with worry, worried about how to keep my family safe, and NOBODY THOUGHT TO TELL ME? I'm calling the police."

"No, David." Mum repeated what Zoran had said to me, that there was no point.

Jas whimpered. "Don't be scared," I whispered to her. "You can see Mum isn't."

"I knew you'd react like this," Mum told Dad. "That's why I didn't tell you. You were so worried."

"Me too," I said. "I'm sorry, Daddy."

"I thought you might stop me seeing Zach," Flora said.

Zach, speaking for the first time, said, "I'm really, really sorry, Mr. Gadsby."

Flora really should have learned by now not to put ideas into Dad's head. Dad looked from Flora to Zach and back at Flora again, and said, "Well you were right, that's exactly what I am going to do. You two are not to see each other."

Mum said, "David, that hardly seems fair," and Dad said he didn't care about being fair, and was he the only one here to appreciate the full gravity of the situation? "That woman is still on the loose," he said, not noticing Zach flinch. "And she is a danger to my family."

"But it's not Zach's fault!" Flora protested.

"I don't care!" Dad roared.

"Daddy!"

"He's right, Flora," said Zach. I wouldn't have thought it was possible, but he looked even paler than before.

"But it's not your fault!" Flora repeated. She squared her shoulders and faced Dad. "You can't stop me! I'm seventeen years old and . . ."

Dad held up his hand to silence her. "Zach, you are a gentleman," he said. "And now, if you all don't mind, I am going for a walk."

He was very dignified as he left the room. I slipped out after him and asked him if he would like company on his walk, but he said, still dignified, that he would rather be alone. He walked down the stairs with his head held high. In the hall, he put on his coat, his scarf, and his old hat. He slipped out of his indoor shoes and pulled on his sneakers.

"AGGGGGGGGhhhhhhhhhhhhhhhhhhhh!"

I swear his scream made the house shake, and his swearing afterward would have made a pirate blush.

Apparently Ron had been using his shoes as a toilet again.

"Those ★★★★★★★ ★★★★★★ cats!" Dad yelled. He pulled off his sneakers and hurled them out into the street. Tore down to the basement for some clean socks. Stormed back upstairs, put on the socks, his shoes, and walked out slamming the door.

Dinner was silent. Dad made pasta with a jar of puttanesca sauce, and even though Jas hates olives, she ate the whole thing without complaining. Mum stayed in bed. Flora stayed in her room. Ron and Hermione stayed in the shed.

FRIDAY, JANUARY 24

Flora skipped school today to see Zach. He called her late last night to ask her to meet him, and she asked me to cover for her. She said, looking more serious than I have ever seen her, not to ask any questions but that things had changed since Wednesday. We left home together this morning as usual, but after we dropped Jas and Twig off we both went in separate directions.

I went to the school office to tell them Flora was sick.

She went to spend the day with Zach and his mother.

She told me everything this afternoon when she got back.

Zach finally heard from his mum last night. She said she wanted to see him, and he thought it would be good for Flora to go too.

Flora said, "But what if she attacks me?" and Zach said that wasn't going happen, and that he wanted his mum to see how great Flora was.

"Once she knows you a bit, she'll love you," Zach said.

"That was a bit deluded," I remarked, and Flora agreed, but she went anyway.

She met him at the train station and they walked down to the river hand in hand. "Does she know I'm coming?" Flora asked, and Zach replied, "Yes, of course, and she thinks it's a really good idea."

It was a beautiful day. They walked past a little park and some pubs and a houseboat with a dog on the roof and a woman watering potted plants and it was all really pretty, except Flora was too nervous to enjoy it. They came to a tiny street with gardens on one side and gardens giving way to the river on the other, and Zach finally stopped in front of a big house with black-and-white marble steps going up to a dark red door and said, "Well, this is where I live; this is my grandparents' house."

"What was it like?" I asked.

"The house? Old, a bit like a museum." Old furniture, and old books, and a kitchen which reminds me of Grandma's, except not as big. Loads of photographs of Zach and his gran. Only one of him and Wanda. But we didn't stay long. Zach called out for his mum and she didn't answer, so he said maybe she was outside, and we crossed the road to the garden.

The garden, Flora says, was like going into another world. They closed the big red front door behind them, went back down the black-and-white steps, crossed the tiny street, and went through an iron gate set inside a tall hedge. Flora says it was like going into Narnia or something, and she could hardly even hear the city anymore. There was a lawn with an old stone bench and a weeping willow tree, with a little wall at the end with another gate in it, and a small jetty on the other side, and on the pontoon there was a little table covered with food, an ice bucket with a bottle of champagne, glasses and cups and plates, and a thermos of coffee, and one of those little barbecues in a bucket, and cakes and croissants and pastries and the smell of cooking sausages. There was jazz music playing.

"Surprise!" Zach's mother appeared suddenly from behind the branches of the weeping willow. Zach started to laugh. Flora tried not to stare.

For today's picnic, Wanda was dressed like a society lady from the 1920s, with a cloche hat and a big fur-collared coat over a drop waist dress, gray buttoned shoes, and matching gloves. She twirled to show herself off.

"Do you like it?" she asked. "I've got something for you too. I thought we should have fun!"

And that was how Flora found herself having the strangest picnic, sitting on a pontoon on the Thames at the end of January, with a feather boa round her neck and a cloche hat of her own, eating croissants and sausages and drinking champagne, with Zach sitting next to her in a straw boater and a striped blazer.

"I didn't know if we should have breakfast or lunch," Wanda said. "So I made brunch!"

She made it sound like brunch was something she had just invented all on her own.

"Did she even mention Mum?" I asked, and Flora said no, but that at this point everything was so strange and rather wonderful she wasn't even thinking about Mum either. That came later, Flora said.

After they'd eaten, Wanda taught Zach and Flora to dance the Charleston, still on the pontoon. Then when the wind started to whip up on the river, they carried everything back to the garden and sat under the willow tree, where she and Zach reminisced about all the other picnics they'd had there, and she made Flora laugh by telling stories of the scrapes Zach got into when he was little.

"You see," Zach said, putting his arm round Flora's shoulders. "I knew you two would get along."

"There was a flash in her eye," Flora said. "An actual flash. Zach didn't see it because he is so besotted with her, but I did. And that is when I remembered Mum."

Wanda said, speaking of Flora, "She's charming, Zach. I'm so glad I got the chance to meet her before I go away tomorrow." Zach said, "What do you mean, before you go away tomorrow?" and Wanda said she had been invited to go and stay with some friends in northern Spain who owned a delightful hotel up in the mountains.

"But you've only just got back from France!" Zach said.

"I'm afraid it can't be helped, my darling," Wanda replied. "I'm sailing on tomorrow's boat. That's why I wanted to see you today."

"Who goes to Spain by boat?" I asked.

"Loads of people, apparently," Flora said. "That's kind of not the point."

"But what about me?" Zach asked when Wanda said about the boat, and Flora's blood started to boil because he looked so miserable. "Where will I live?"

Wanda replied that Zach seemed to be very happy living where he was.

"I can't stay with Zoran forever," Zach said.

"Can't you stay here on your own?"

"No," Flora snapped. "He can't."

"You're my family, Mum," Zach insisted.

"Well your grandfather doesn't seem to think so," Wanda said.

"And that's when I left," Flora concluded. "I couldn't stand it. She really is a witch, Blue. She puts spells on people. She almost put a spell on *me*, with her music and her clothes and her fancy picnic. His little face when she said that she was leaving again! He walked me back to the end of the street, and I tried to tell him what she was doing but he wouldn't listen. I said she was playing us, him against his grandfather, him against me. I said she doesn't care about anyone but herself, she only told you about Spain because you were talking about me and she can't stand it not being all about her."

"What did Zach say?"

"That I was wrong and that she loves him. Didn't I see how she was today? Would she really put on a picnic like that if she didn't love him, if she didn't want to impress me? I said she'd have impressed me more if she'd bothered to apologize about hurling stones at my mother."

"How did he react to that?"

"He said we have to look after her. I said, no, *you* have to look after her. She's not my problem, and maybe Dad's right, maybe we shouldn't see each other for a while. I told him to call me when he'd gotten over his mother complex, and that I was going back to my own family."

"You said that? Call me when you're over your mother complex?"

Flora gave a tiny smile. "It's not quite a milk shake, but seriously, I'm tired of always hearing about her. I can't believe I ever thought it was more important to protect Zach than tell the truth to Dad. There's no one more important than you all, no one."

Sometimes I really love my big sister, but she is always so extreme.

"I can't believe Wanda never mentioned Mum to you," I said. "And I'm really pleased you stood up for us and everything, but don't you think that now *you* are being unfair to Zach?"

Flora looked worried. "Do you think so?"

"A little bit."

"I'll call him tomorrow," she said. "He'll need cheering

up anyway if that witch really is leaving. Also, do you think I should tell Dad what happened today? I'm tired of secrets. And Jas will be relieved to know Wanda's leaving."

"He'll be furious with you for disobeying him, but yeah, I think you should."

"I'll go right now, before I lose my nerve." She opened the door. The sound of Dad and Jas yelling at each other floated up from the kitchen. Flora caught my eye and we both started to laugh.

"Maybe not right now," I suggested.

I grabbed my camera and together we tiptoed downstairs to see what was going on.

THE FILM DIARIES OF BLUEBELL GADSBY
SCENE EIGHT (TRANSCRIPT)
THE HEADLESS CORPSE
OR THE INEVITABLE OUTCOME OF RELEASING YOUR PETS

INTERIOR. DAY. THE GADSBY HOUSE.

Screaming grows louder as CAMERAMAN (BLUE) enters the kitchen, where DAD is holding RON and HERMIONE by the scruff of the neck. JASMINE jumps up and down around him trying to catch the kittens, who contort their bodies as they seek to escape, meowing piteously. On the floor lie the smashed remains of a fruit bowl, two kitchen chairs, several oranges, a squashed banana, and a decapitated baby rat. TWIG sits on the sofa, watching in awed fascination.

JAS

(screams)

IT'S YOUR FAULT! IT'S YOUR FAULT! YOU
SHOULDN'T HAVE LET THEM GO!!

DAD

(also screams)

YOU HAVE NO WAY OF KNOWING THESE ARE
YOUR BABY RATS. THEY COULD BE ANY BABY
RATS!! AND ANYWAY, IT WASN'T ME WHO
KILLED THEM!!!

JAS

(roars)

BETSY WAS PREGNANT WHEN YOU LET HER
ESCAPE! WHY ELSE WOULD THERE BE BABY
RATS IN OUR GARDEN?

TWIG

Face it, Dad, you pulled the trigger yourself.

JAS and DAD
SHUT UP, TWIG!

DAD

(a little more calmly)

It is *not* my fault that this house is overrun by

rodents and murderous felines.

JAS

(snarls)

This would never have happened if they were safe

in their cage!

FLORA

(entering kitchen after Blue)

OH MY GOD, THERE'S A RAT WITHOUT A HEAD!!

Flora joins the debris on the floor in a dead faint. Dad

drops the kittens and starts to slap her. The kittens

pounce on the dead baby rat and drag it, snarling, un-

der the dresser.

DAD

I want those creatures gone by tonight.

JAS

(now hysterical)

Daddy, please!

FLORA

(returns to consciousness)

Where am I?

DAD

IF THEY'RE NOT GONE BY MORNING, I WILL
TAKE THEM TO THE PET SHOP! FIRST MY SHOES
AND NOW A HEADLESS CORPSE!! WHAT IS
WRONG WITH THIS FAMILY? CAN NO ONE ELSE
SEE HOW WRONG THIS IS???

FRIDAY, JANUARY 24 (CONT.)

Dad's phone rang then and he stopped yelling because it
was Mum calling from upstairs, telling him to stop shouting
and also asking for a cup of tea. Flora staggered across to the
sofa and said she felt sick and wanted tea too. Twig passed
her a bucket. Jas sat down next to her and glared at Dad
until he left.

"I thought he liked the kittens now," she said.

"I don't think he likes anyone or anything right at the
moment," Flora said.

"Do you think he really will take them to the pet shop?"

"I think he's almost as mad as Zach's mother," Flora replied.

Twig started doing angry Dad impersonations, scratching under his arms like a monkey and going, "I've got fleas! Who pooped in my shoes?"

"It's not funny," said Jas.

"I've had a brilliant idea," I said.

They all turned toward me, looking expectant. I do love it when they do that.

"We'll take them to Gloria," I announced.

"That's your brilliant idea?" said Twig. "Are you sure she likes kittens?"

"They can be stable cats," I said. "They'd love that Jas. They're half wild anyway, and you can visit them every week. You know if they stay here, they'll only keep on hunting down the rats. This way, the babies will get to grow up, *and* the kittens will be happy."

Jas said my idea *was* brilliant, and that if Ron and Hermione couldn't live with us, there was nobody in the world she would rather they live with than Gloria. She wanted to take them right away.

"We'll go tomorrow," I said. "It's already getting dark and I'm not getting murdered in that alley, not even for Ron and Hermione."

"Dad said they had to be gone tonight."

"I've had an idea for that too."

"Not again," groaned Zoran when Jas, Twig, and I turned

213

up at his flat complete with two kittens, their litter tray, and sleeping box. "How many times do I have to say no?"

"One night," I said.

"Dad's banished them," Twig explained.

"Like Zach," Jas added.

"Where is Zach, by the way?" I asked.

Zoran said he was in the shower.

"Is he okay?" I asked.

"Well he's not exactly tap-dancing and singing show tunes, but he's doing all right. Why?"

"Nothing," I said.

If Zach hasn't told Zoran about seeing his mum, there's no way I'm getting involved.

Back home, I told Dad our plans about the kittens. I thought maybe he would grant a last-minute reprieve, like they do in books, but he didn't. Jas has also appealed to Mum one last time, but Mum says she doesn't want to upset Dad.

Zoran is meeting us tomorrow at the train station.

THE FILM DIARIES OF BLUEBELL GADSBY
SCENE NINE (TRANSCRIPT)
KITTEN HANDOVER

EXTERIOR. DAY. STREET SCENE, OUTSIDE A TRAIN
STATION.

ZORAN stands waiting at the entrance to the train station, holding a cardboard box, from which loud meows
and hisses emit. Passersby glance at him curiously.
Zoran wears a thick leather jacket, leather gloves, and
motorcycle boots. There is a vivid red scratch on his
left cheek.

JASMINE takes the box from him and coos at it. Zoran
glares at it malevolently. The box hisses louder.

> ZORAN
> Are you sure Gloria is going to want these
> horrors?

TWIG

Personally, I have my doubts.

JASMINE

(offended)

They are not horrors.

CAMERAMAN (BLUE)

(with fake breeziness)

Everybody loves kittens. Are you coming with us?

ZORAN

I feel I should. I'd feel responsible if anything
happened to you on the train with those charming
creatures in tow.

Cut to entrance of the stable yard. Zoran, Twig, Jas,
Cameraman, and cardboard box are gathered outside
the gate. The sky is bright blue and their breath comes
out in little frozen puffs. Even the alleyway looks almost
pretty in the sunshine. A clump of snowdrops has come
out in the tiny patch of earth under the chestnut tree.

CAMERAMAN

(still being positive)

Nothing bad can happen on a day like today.

As one body, they turn into the yard, where ponies hang their heads over their boxes. BILL sits checking the straps on riding hats. GLORIA strides about looking splendid in skintight jodhpurs, drinking coffee and carrying a pitchfork.

Zoran gazes at her.

GLORIA

(kindly, to Jas, not appearing to notice Zoran)

You're a little early for your lesson, aren't you? What's in the box?

JAS

(suddenly unsure, casting imploring glances at Cameraman)

They're um . . . well . . . sort of . . .

Box meows loudly.

ZORAN

(still gazing)

We were wondering if you might . . .

CAMERAMAN

We thought in case you had mice . . .

TWIG

They're very good at killing rats.

JASMINE

(glares at Twig, before squaring her shoulders to
announce confidently)

They are my kittens, and I would like them to
come and live with you.

Gloria's mouth twitches. Zoran places the cardboard
box on the floor. Gloria and Bill approach. Jas lifts up
the lid. Two black kitten heads pop up, ears pricked,
green eyes flashing like lightning, oversized whiskers
twitching indignantly. Hermione is the first out. She
leaps cleanly over the top of the box and pads cau-
tiously into the yard, sniffing. Ron, who is fatter and
clumsier, clips the edge of the box, falls to the ground,

turns a somersault, and follows his sister with his short tail held high, like he missed his entrance on purpose.

Camera swings to Gloria. The expression on her face confirms fears that she is not a kitten person. She stares at them, baffled.

> GLORIA
> You're bringing me kittens?

> ZORAN
> (trying to be ingratiating)
> We thought they might be useful.

> GLORIA
> But what am I going to do with . . .

She is interrupted by a new noise, a sort of wheezing, rumbling, spluttering sound, so unexpected it takes a moment to locate where it is coming from.

It is the sound of Bill, laughing.

Bill crouches down. Hermione, sensing a friend, marches up to him and rubs her face against his leg. Ron, not to be outdone, follows. Bill unmistakably coos.

Unlike his daughter, it appears he *is* the kitten type.

> GLORIA
> (face softening at the sight of her father petting kittens)
> Have they had all their vaccinations yet?

Her eyes meet Zoran's for the first time and she blushes.

SATURDAY, JANUARY 25

I'm writing this from the back of the car.

It was sweet, watching Zoran and Gloria connect like that, their eyes locking over a box full of kittens. I kind of wish Dodi had been there. It would have thrilled her romantic heart, but given everything that happened afterward, it feels like it took place almost in another life.

Gloria's blush only lasted about three seconds, but we all saw it.

"We met at the recital," Zoran stammered.

Twig sniggered. I kicked him. Mopsy tried to sniff Hermione who scratched him on the nose; Ron found a corner to wee in; Jas and Bill wandered off into the tack room to find a place for the kittens' bed. And Flora turned up on Zoran's scooter.

"What the ★★★★?" I thought Zoran's eyes were going to pop out of his head, and who can blame him, when one moment he is gazing goofily at Gloria and the next his hot-headed ex-charge, who for all he knows has never ridden a scooter in her life, turns up driving his personal property.

"Never mind all that!" Flora cried. "Zach has disappeared!"

"What do you mean?" cried Zoran.

"He's not answering his phone."

"But that doesn't mean . . ."

"Will you just listen to me!" Flora shouted. Then she clambered off the scooter, took a deep breath, and told us what had happened.

"I argued with Zach yesterday," she said. "But this morning, when I woke up, I wanted to say I was sorry. So I rang him."

Flora being Flora, it wasn't enough for her just to leave a message. Instead, knowing he was working at Vinnie's this morning, she decided to pay him a surprise visit.

"But your father," Zoran said. "You're not supposed to see . . ."

"Please," said Flora.

Even though it was still early, Vinnie was already there, but he told her Zach had called in sick. So then she decided to call on Zach to minister to him on his sickbed but when she got to Zoran's, there was nobody there. She found the emergency key Zoran keeps hidden in a loose brick in the wall for whenever Zach forgets his ("That's supposed to be a secret!" Zoran said, but she ignored him) and let herself into the flat, which is when she saw that Zach's things were gone, his clothes and his guitar and everything. So she panicked, grabbed Zoran's helmet and the keys to his scooter and rode over to Zach's grandfather's house.

"Why would he do that?" Zoran asked.

"In case his mum was there," I explained. "Flora spent the day with them yesterday."

"What! Why does nobody tell me anything?" Zoran sounded exasperated and furious and disappointed all at once.

"He sounds just like Dad," Twig whispered.

"I wanted to last night, but I thought it would be better if Zach did," I explained.

"You saw Zach's mum yesterday?" Jas asked Flora. She looked at me. *And you knew?*

"Is anyone listening to a word I'm saying?" Flora shouted.

"Carry on," ordered Zoran.

"There was nobody at the house. I rang the doorbell, and I checked in the garden, and then I shouted up at the window to Zach's room, and eventually a neighbor came out and said, if I was looking for Zach I was too late, because he had gone. He saw him leave this morning with Wanda and a rucksack and a guitar."

Zoran was looking really confused.

"But he was asleep at home when I left!"

"Did you check on him?" I asked.

"I just assumed," he admitted. Poor Zoran was shaking. Gloria took command.

"Where do you think he has gone?" she demanded.

"SPAIN!" Flora howled. "By boat! Today!"

Twig nodded and said. "The Portsmouth Santander service."

"How do you *know* that?" Gloria asked.

"I have spent a lot of time recently studying transportation," Twig replied.

Zoran looked like he did when he lost Twig on the train last year, only much, much worse. Gloria said, "We have to find out from which station and when trains leave for Portsmouth."

"Trains to Portsmouth Harbor leave from Waterloo," Twig said. "There are trains all the time. The next one leaves at ten, and gets in at eleven thirty-three. Of course, he might have caught the bus, which is cheaper, but slower. I don't know the bus timetables. The ferries leave at different times every day, depending on the tides. If someone gives me a smartphone, I can look up today's sailing time."

"Thank goodness for Maisie's little brother," Zoran muttered as he copied down train times. His phone rang. "Maybe it's Zach," Zoran said hopefully, then he looked at the number. "Oh ★★★★, it's his grandfather."

He walked away from us to take the call.

Gloria raised an eyebrow at me. "Zach is the boy from the performance?"

"Yes."

"And his grandfather?"

"Is in hospital. Zoran is supposed to be looking after Zach."

"And the reason it's a bad thing Zach is with his mother?"

"She's a witch," said Flora. "She keeps running away, and she tried to kill Mum."

"I see," Gloria said. "And are Zach and Zoran related?"

"Not even a little bit," I said. "Zoran's just a very, very nice person."

Gloria smiled.

Zoran came back from talking to Mr. Rudowski, looking shaken but also quite determined. "He wanted to know if we'd found his daughter."

"What did he say when you said you'd lost his grand-son?" asked Twig.

"He was understandably very upset," Zoran said. "This time he said we should call the police."

"And tell them what?" Gloria asked. "That a boy has run away with his mother?"

"It's all my fault!" cried Flora. "I was mean to him! Zoran, you have to do something! He can't run away with her, she's evil!"

"I don't think she's evil," Zoran said slowly. "But I agree he can't go with her."

He was holding his phone to his ear again. "Straight to answerphone." He started tapping out a text.

"How can you text at a time like this!"

I've never seen Flora so hysterical.

"It's important. He might read a text, even if he's not answering his phone."

"We have to *do* something, Zoran!" Flora begged

"Yes, but what?" Zoran said.

"Find him of course," said Bill. Everyone turned around and looked at him like he was mad, or a genius, or maybe both.

"How?" asked Zoran.

Unlike Dad, Bill copes beautifully in a crisis.

"The train station, the bus station, and the harbor," he

said. "Chances are he's left town already, but you never know. Gloria'll take Waterloo, I'll go to Victoria, you get yourself down to Portsmouth."

"By train?" Zoran looked confused.

"Don't be daft, man! By bike!"

We all looked a little bit skeptically across to where Zoran's electric scooter was parked under the chestnut tree.

"Not that thing!" Bill grunted. He shuffled across the yard to the box right at the end of the row and threw the doors open. Inside stood what I have since discovered is a gleaming vintage Harley-Davidson.

"Mine, from a long time ago," Bill said. "Still goes like the wind, though you'll have to top up the fuel. You'd better get going."

"But you? How will you get to Waterloo? To Victoria? By train?"

Bill laughed then, a real laugh, not a wheeze.

"How do you think we'll get there?" he roared. "On horseback!"

And suddenly they were all running around like headless chickens.

"I'm coming with you!" Flora yelled as Zoran pulled his helmet on.

"I cannot take responsibility . . ."

"Bill, have you got a spare helmet? Leathers? Can I have some riding boots?"

"You go to Victoria, Gloria, I'll take Waterloo!"

"Flora," I said, "oh, for God's sake, just get on!"

"I called my friend Penny who helps me sometimes," Gloria cried, dashing past with a bridle and saddle. "She'll be here in about twenty minutes. Until then I'm leaving you kids in charge."

Zoran gazed at her in admiration.

"Move!" Flora screeched.

They were all gone in less than ten minutes, in a cloud of diesel fumes and a clatter of hooves. I'm not sure it's good for horses to gallop down streets. I'm pretty certain it's illegal. But I do know I've never seen Bill look so happy.

"Do you think he really did used to be a jockey?" Jas sat on the floor, cuddling Ron and Hermione, while Flopsy nibbled her sweatshirt.

"Looks like it," I said.

"Who do you think will find him?" asked Twig.

We started to try to guess—Gloria, because she's so cool! Bill, because he's the fastest!—but our conversation was cut short when our car shrieked into the yard and Dad threw open the door, demanding to know why he had just seen Flora riding off down the street on the back of a motorbike.

I had to stop writing because I was feeling sick. I have never been so fast in a car, ever.

It only took Dad about five minutes to get the whole story out of us. The minute he heard what Flora and Zoran were doing, he yelled that he was going after them. Then he realized he had no idea how to get to Portsmouth Harbor, and needed Twig to go with him because Twig is the only one who understands how to use the SatNav. I said I wanted to go too, which meant Jas also had to come because she's too small to be left alone.

"But we have to wait for Penny," Jas said, partly because she is a very responsible stable hand but also because she was buying time for Zoran and Flora to get away.

Once we were finally off, Dad drove like a lunatic, yelling out random sentences like, "I only came to find you because I felt bad about the kittens!" and "Spain! Portsmouth! Motorbikes! Jesus!" and "WhyOWhyOWhy are we having another baby?"

"I still don't understand why we are going after them," Twig said as we roared onto the motorway.

"They might have an accident!" Dad shouted. "Zach's mother is a maniac! Flora might run away to Spain! ANYTHING MIGHT HAPPEN!"

Dad swerved to avoid a lorry. Twig screamed.

"I am just doing what any parent would do!" Dad yelled.

"Is Daddy being a hero?" Jas whispered to me.

"In a way," I whispered back.

We caught up with Zoran and Flora as they pulled out of a gas station on the motorway.

"I thought motorbikes were really fast," Jas remarked. "How come they're not farther ahead?"

"Zoran is a very responsible driver," I said. Dad gave a short laugh, swerved again and swore.

"You can't slow down," Twig told him. "The ferry sails in less than an hour."

We kept them in our sights right up until the turnoff for Portsmouth, but we lost them in the queue to the harbor, mainly because Zoran managed to avoid the traffic by riding his motorbike down the oncoming lane, which was empty. Then, when we arrived at the entrance to the harbor, Dad had to explain that we were looking for the ferry to Spain, but that we didn't have any tickets and nor did we want to buy any.

"I am looking for my daughter!" Dad cried. "She has run away on a motorbike to find her boyfriend."

The ticket man, whose badge said he was called Percy Williams, said that was the most exciting thing he'd heard all day, but that boarding for the *Queen Sofia* had already closed.

"We're too late!" Jas wailed.

"Let us through!" Dad snarled at Percy. "My daughter is somewhere in this precinct and I mean to bring her home!"

Percy said he sympathized because he also had daughters, but in his experience there was not a blind bit of use trying to stop them falling in love with unsuitable boyfriends.

"You've just got to let it run its course," Percy advised. Behind us, a long line of cars were honking their horns. "I'm going to have to ask you to leave now."

Dad reversed out of the line, parked the car on the side of the road, and tore back past Percy's hut at a sprint, with the rest of us right behind him. Quite a few people were watching by now and a group of kids on a school trip even started to cheer.

"There's no more boat until tomorrow!" Percy shouted after us, but Dad didn't listen. He ran, and we ran after him, all the way to the waterfront, and then he stopped so suddenly we all bumped into him, because there, sitting on a pillar on the quayside, looking out to sea with his rucksack at his feet and his guitar still on his back, watching the *Queen Sofia* pull out of Portsmouth Harbor, was Zach. And there also, walking toward him, clad in leather and carrying their helmets and looking like something out of a Hollywood movie, were Zoran and Flora.

Zach looked up when he heard footsteps behind him.

Zoran and Flora both reached out to touch him. Zach said something we couldn't hear. Flora flung her arms around him. Zoran put his arms around them both.

Dad sniffed loudly.

Jas announced, "Daddy, I don't care what you say about us not being allowed to talk to Zach," and marched over toward the hugging, huddled heap that was Zach and Zoran and Flora. Twig and I followed.

"You missed the boat," Jas said.

"No, I didn't," Zach whispered.

Like Grandma says, there's always a choice. Zach's choice was whether to leave or stay. And when he switched his phone back on and read Zoran's text, he made his decision.

Zoran's text said: "Ask Wanda to tell you the truth about why she left you."

So he did. And I don't know what he said to her, but for once Wanda did tell him the truth.

After Zach's Gran died, Mr. Rudowski gave Wanda a choice: stay at home with them and get medical help, or leave. He said if she stayed he would help her, but that things couldn't go on as they had before, that it wasn't fair to Zach.

"The doctors would have put me on drugs," Wanda told Zach. "I didn't want that."

Mr. Rudowski didn't kick her out. Wanda chose to leave.

"Witch," Flora said fiercely.

"She's not a witch," Zach said softly. "She's frightened."

Flora snorted. Zoran frowned at her and she stopped.

"But why did you run away?" Jas wanted to know.

"She asked me to go with her." Zach said.

Suddenly I remembered how lost he looked at Zoran's concert, when he realized Wanda hadn't come after all. I pictured him as a little boy, laughing with his mum at one of her crazy picnics. And then I thought of him and Mr. Rudowski, living alone in the old house by the river, both missing people who weren't there, and I understood.

I guess a part of Zach will always want to be with his mum.

So Zach left. He went home to Zoran's flat, said nothing, waited till Zoran was sleeping, and crept back to his grandfather's house in the early morning.

"I was going to do it," he said. "All the way down on the train Mum kept talking about the mountains, about fig and apricot and almond trees, goats and beaches and blue sky. I knew even then that it was crazy, but she made it sound wonderful. Then we arrived, and I switched on my phone, and there was Zoran's text. After Mum told me the truth, all I could think about was Grandad. He lied for her. He let me believe he'd kicked her out so I didn't know she'd chosen to leave me. And he's old and sick, he's completely lost without

Grandma, and I've been so angry with him. So I said I wasn't going with her. And Mum—Mum decided to leave."

Zach's voice wobbled, but he didn't cry. Flora hugged him even closer.

"I'm sorry," she said.

"Me too," he replied. "As someone very wise once explained to me—it's the people who stay who really matter."

He looked at me when he said that, and I felt all happy inside.

Far out at sea, the *Queen Sofia* had disappeared. We were all watching it: Twig, Jas, and me with our feet dangling over the water, Zach on one pillar with his arms around Flora, Zoran on another. It was a big moment.

"The ones who stay, and the ones who come after you."

Dad had crept up on us without any of us hearing.

"I'm glad you stayed, son," he said.

Slowly, slowly, Zach smiled his amazing smile.

"Come on," Zoran said. "I'll buy you all something to eat."

We turned our backs on the sea and walked across the empty quayside to the entrance to the embarkation lot.

"No way is that yours!" Zach said, when we stopped at Bill's Harley.

"It's a long story," Zoran said.

Twig's phone rang while we were arguing about who should ride into town with Zoran. "It's for you," he said, handing me the phone. "It's that mad cow you call your best friend."

"Tell Twig I heard that," Dodi said. "And where *are* you?"

"Portsmouth," I grinned.

"What? Where even *is* that? Listen, Jake's had an idea."

I let Dodi talk. Flora and Zach were sitting together on the motorbike. Dad was on the phone to Mum, trying to explain what had happened, and Jas was talking to Gloria on Zoran's phone. Flora wrapped her arms around Zach and whispered something in his ear. They both laughed. The sun was shining. The sea was blue. It was perfect.

"Tomorrow then," Dodi was saying.

"Sure," I smiled, and gave the phone back to Twig.

Zoran rode into town with Zach, and we all followed behind.

THE FILM DIARIES OF BLUEBELL GADSBY
SCENE TEN (TRANSCRIPT)
CRIMINAL ACTIVITY

EXTERIOR. PREDAWN. THE PLAYGROUND OF CLAREN-
DON FREE SCHOOL.

JAKE, COLIN, SAM, DODI, and CAMERAMAN (BLUE)
have just scaled the school gates and huddle beneath
the window of the staff common room.

>CAMERAMAN (BLUE)
>Won't it be locked?

>JAKE
>(proud of himself)
>Shouldn't be. I slipped in during Saturday
>detention and stole the window bolts.

>CAMERAMAN
>But isn't there an alarm?

DODI

Blue, stop being so *negative*! Jake's thought of
everything! He's got thirty seconds before it goes
off.

CAMERAMAN

Thirty seconds!

JAKE

(assuming the air of a commando officer and
brandishing a pair of wire cutters)
All right, lads. I'm going in.

Colin gives him a leg up to the windowsill. Jake
crouches on the ledge. It looks for a moment as if he
will lose his balance and fall, but then he grins down
at his friends on the ground and they realize that he
is showing off. He pushes the sash open and reaches
down for the camera.

CAMERAMAN (JAKE)

And so our intrepid explorer ventures into the
scary depths of the Staff Common Room. This is
the den where Math teachers lurk, the natural
habitat of child-eating French teachers . . . And

here, if our bold adventurer is not mistaken, is
said French teacher's locker.

Picture is reduced to blurred image of common room
floor as Jake fumbles in his rucksack. Off camera,
there is the sound of heavy breathing, and a sharp
click as metal cutters cut through a padlock.

CAMERAMAN (JAKE)
Eureka!

A pair of gloved hands picks through the contents of
the locker—books, notebooks, a printed scarf, perfume,
two bottles of Evian, a packet of crackers, and a cardboard box containing lipsticks, tissues, and an assort-
ment of confiscated telephones. Jake grabs the lot and
stuffs them into his rucksack. The screech of a burglar
alarm splits the air. Picture goes mad as Jake vaults
out of the window.

CAMERAMAN (JAKE)
RUN!

I've never run so fast or laughed so much while I was running. We raced to the school gate, scrambled over it, and kept on running until we reached the park, where we collapsed on a bench, panting and still laughing. Jake reached into his rucksack and pulled out Madame Gilbert's box of lipsticks and telephones.

"One of these is yours, I believe, milady," he said.

"I can't believe you just did that!" I said, taking the box.

"Anything for you, Blue," Jake said, and that is when I noticed the way that Dodi was looking at him, like he was some kind of superhero.

Dodi likes Jake. I can't believe I never realized before.

Mum came downstairs today. Now that Dad has developed a taste for being heroic, he wanted to carry her down from her bedroom, but she wouldn't let him. Instead he has been driving her mad with his fussing, but you can see that she actually loves it. And Zoran came around on his way back from the stables. His excuse for going over was to pick up his scooter and also to pay the fines Gloria and Bill got for galloping their horses across London looking for Zach, but when he came back he couldn't stop grinning.

Gloria is going to give him riding lessons.

As for Zach, he has finished writing his song for Flora. He played it to her this afternoon in the tree house, and when they came down her eyes were shining. Zach says he's going to play it at Zoran's next concert, but I'm not allowed to film it. And my point about all this is these people, one way or another, are all in love. And however many telephones Jake steals for me or how many roses he gives me, nothing is going to change the fact that I just don't feel that way about him. So this afternoon I went around to Jake's house and did something I should have done a long time ago.

"If it's because of Talullah," Jake said, "I promise that is completely over."

"It's not about Talullah," I said. Then, because I had promised myself I was going to be truthful, I added, "I mean it's not *completely* about Talullah. I just don't want to go out with you. I never *did* want to go out with you in the first place. I only said yes because it felt a bit awkward to say no, which if you think about it is a completely rubbish basis for a relationship. You're amazing because you're the sort of brilliant person who is prepared to break into school to steal back a telephone, but please can we just be friends again?"

It all came out in a rush and I did feel a bit bad because

of the criminal activity and everything, but I think he finally got the message. Afterward I went around to Dodi's house to tell her. I could see she was secretly pleased, but she said, "You're mad, everyone wants a boyfriend."

"Well I am not everyone," I said.

"I bet this time next week you'll be back together with him."

I didn't have a milk shake handy, but there was a bottle of water on the table. "You wouldn't dare," Dodi said, but I did. I chased her all round her garden with it and only stopped when she was so wet you could see her bra through her T-shirt.

Boys can wait. Friends are way more fun.

SATURDAY, MARCH 8

People only write in diaries when things are going badly. And lately things have been good.

I had a long chat with Dodi after I'd spoken to Jake, and she admitted that she has liked him for ages, ever since she spent so much time talking to him about me. She said she would never go out with him if I minded even the tiniest bit. I told her that I would mind a *lot* if she didn't. They have been together for nearly a month now, and they really are the cutest couple. Now that Jake has found a girl who adores him and who doesn't live in a different hemisphere, he has become the model boyfriend.

Zoran and Gloria—well, let's just say their relationship has extended to beyond riding lessons.

Ron and Hermione kill every rodent that crosses their paths at the stables. Which is nice for them, if not for the rodents.

Jas and Bill have become best friends and are writing poetry together.

Twig finally understood Maisie Carter was just using him as a free babysitting service, and is now pining for a new girl called Bianca.

Flora and Zach are more in love than ever, and Mr. Rudowski has come home.

Me? There's nothing new. And that's just fine. Life's good. Boring. No surprises.

EXCEPT TODAY!!!!

TODAY WAS VERY, VERY, VERY EXCITING.

Today, for the first time, we met Mr. Rudowski.

THE FILM DIARIES OF BLUEBELL GADSBY
SCENE ELEVEN (TRANSCRIPT)
MR. RUDOWSKI COMES FOR DINNER

INTERIOR, EVENING, 32 CHATSWORTH SQUARE.

On the top floor, FLORA paces her bedroom, trying on and throwing down clothes, wailing things like *What shall I wear? I have no clothes! OH, what am I supposed to wear?* Pan to kitchen, where MOTHER moves heavily about the kitchen. For once, the kitchen is not a mess. A stew bubbles gently on the stove. A salad nestles in a bowl on the table, which is perfectly set with mostly unchipped china. A pan of boiled potatoes sits on the side, waiting to be mashed. Mother grunts as she bends down to check on the pineapple cake in the oven. "Perfect," she murmurs. She waddles over to the sofa and falls asleep.

Pan to study where FATHER sits hunched over his laptop, typing with a look of furious concentration.

Pan to landing, where TWIG sits on the floor, practicing card tricks on JAS.

JAS
Do you really think card tricks are going to impress her?

TWIG
Everybody loves card tricks.

Front door bell rings. Flora appears on the landing, wearing a navy blue trouser suit, sensible shoes, a silk scarf around her neck, and a slash of fuchsia lipstick.

FLORA
How do I look?

JAS
(awestruck)
Really, really *boring.*

TWIG
Except for the lipstick. The lipstick makes you look mad.

Downstairs, Mother (now awake) has opened the door to ZORAN, GLORIA, ZACH, and MR. RUDOWSKI. Mr. Rudowski wears a hat, a natty blazer, and a spotted bow tie. Gloria is magnificent in her usual skintight black and glossy knee-high boots.

MR. RUDOWSKI
(raises Mother's hand to his lips)
Mrs. Gadsby, thank you so much for inviting me to dinner. I have heard so much about you from Zach.

ZACH
(looks up, spots Flora on the landing)
Flora, come and meet Grandpa!

FLORA
(wailing)
I can't, I have to get changed!

FATHER
(bursts out of study)
I finished my book! I finished my book!

The fire alarm goes off. Black smoke begins to waft up from the kitchen.

MOTHER

I forgot the cake!

ZORAN

(to Mr. Rudowski)

I'm afraid they're often like this.

Mother starts to waddle toward the kitchen but suddenly stops with a startled squeak. All turn to look at her. She stands in a state of shock, looking down at her bump.

MOTHER

I think my water has broken!

FATHER

Call the midwife! Put the kettle on! Where are my car keys?

He runs upstairs, shouting something about Mother's hospital bag. Mother watches him go and smiles. Then, as her first contraction starts, she winces. The contraction passes. She smiles again.

MOTHER

Turn the camera off, Blue.